Now, holding the tiny being that belonged to her, opening the blanket to count fingers and toes, Jesse experienced a new level of awe, even if baby Allie did sleep through the whole examination. "She's beautiful."

"Prettiest baby in the hospital," Brock agreed. "She takes after her mama."

He tucked a burnished red curl behind her ear. "How are you doing?"

"My baby's here." She flashed him a half-shy glance. "You're here. I've never been better."

Dear Reader,

I read my first romance when I was twelve.
I was shopping with my mother and I begged and
pleaded for her to spend fifteen cents to buy me
this pretty pink book in a special display at the
front of the store. An attractive couple faced off on
the cover and the back teased me with the prospect
of a marriage of convenience. My mother gave in,
and I've never looked back. In fact, my latest story,
Her Baby, His Proposal, is a marriage-of-convenience
story. What an honor if it catches the imagination of
a young reader.

Harlequin Romance® celebrates life, family and the
power of love. I admire and respect this genre of
fiction because no matter the hardship or loss the
characters suffer, they choose to fight, to survive
and to triumph.

Teresa Carpenter

TERESA CARPENTER

Her Baby, His Proposal

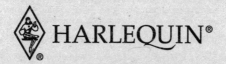

TORONTO • NEW YORK • LONDON
AMSTERDAM • PARIS • SYDNEY • HAMBURG
STOCKHOLM • ATHENS • TOKYO • MILAN • MADRID
PRAGUE • WARSAW • BUDAPEST • AUCKLAND

ISBN-13: 978-0-373-17522-2
ISBN-10:   0-373-17522-1

HER BABY, HIS PROPOSAL

First North American Publication 2008.

Copyright © 2008 by Teresa Carpenter.

This edition published by arrangement with Harlequin Books S.A.

® and TM are trademarks of the publisher. Trademarks indicated with ® are registered in the United States Patent and Trademark Office, the Canadian Trade Marks Office and in other countries.

www.eHarlequin.com

Printed in U.S.A.

From bump to baby and beyond....

Whether she's expecting or they're adopting, a special arrival is on its way!

Follow the tears and triumphs as these couples find their lives blessed with the magic of parenthood....

Look out for more bumps and babies coming soon to Harlequin Romance®.

Next month:
Adopted: Outback Baby
by Barbara Hannay

With her baby grandson in need of her care and her former sweetheart back in town, Nell finds, at the age of thirty-nine, she may finally become a wife and mother....

Teresa Carpenter believes in the power of unconditional love and that there's no better place to find it than between the pages of a romance novel. Reading is a passion for Teresa, a passion that led to a calling. She began writing more than twenty years ago and marks the sale of her first book as one of her happiest memories. Teresa gives back to her craft by volunteering her time to Romance Writers of America on a local and national level. A fifth generation Californian, she lives in San Diego within miles of her extensive family and knows with their help she can accomplish anything. She takes particular joy and pride in her nieces and nephews who are all bright, fit, shining stars of the future. If she's not at a family event, you'll usually find her at home reading, writing, or playing with her adopted Chihuahua, Jefe.

CHAPTER ONE

Hey Babe,
It's been fun but it's over. I can't be a father. Like you
keep telling me, I haven't grown up yet myself. Have
a happy future. Good luck with the kid.
Tad
P.S. I used Tracy's computer to set up online banking
for you and took the money you owed me. Your
password is *goodbye*.

JESSE Manning pulled the sticky note off the unopened
early pregnancy test and crushed it in her fist.

Message received.

With a sick feeling of dread she rushed to Tracy's
computer, booted up and logged on to her bank account.
He'd cleaned her out.

He'd left her. Taken her money and left her alone
and possibly, probably, oh-God-she-prayed-she-wasn't
pregnant.

Dragging in a deep breath, she swept her red hair behind her ears and tried to regroup.

She hadn't owed Tad any money. As always he'd owed her. A half-hysterical laugh escaped her tear-clogged throat. How ironic that he was the one who had always chided her for keeping her money in a shoebox rather than the bank. And when she finally followed his advice, he wiped her out in one swipe.

On top of that Tracy had hit her up this morning for $150 because she was short on the rent. Tad's fond farewell along with Tracy's shortage left Jesse reeling, emotions and finances both strained to the breaking point.

She called the bank to see if she could reverse the transaction. They advised her to put the complaint in writing and contact the police regarding the theft.

She would, too.

No more protecting Tad, no more making excuses for him. He'd gone too far this time.

His desertion didn't surprise her. His timing could have been better, but in reality, they'd been over for a long time. But this time he hadn't just taken from her, he could potentially have stolen from his child.

She'd made a break a year ago when she'd left him and the Midwest behind for a new beginning in San Diego. Her mistake was in believing he'd changed when he'd shown up on her doorstep three months ago.

Her spirits sank further as she realized he'd stolen her dream along with her money. Again. She wanted to teach, and had been saving for tuition and books while she gained California residency status.

Now she'd have to start saving all over again.

Ignoring the pregnancy test—she had neither the time nor the strength for that right now—she ran a brush through her hair, then reached for her mascara before running to catch the bus. She wouldn't be sorry Tad was gone, wouldn't regret the loss of a man too shallow to see she was the best thing that ever happened to him.

Working the tables at the Green Garter, a bar and grill not far from the 32nd Street Navy pier, she brooded on Tad's disappearance and the thin state of her bank account. So, when Stan told her he was short-staffed, she wearily agreed to a double shift.

"Hey, red," a voice called out, "we need another round over here."

Clenching her teeth at the stale, hated nickname, Jesse nodded to indicate she'd heard. She caught her manager's eye from behind the bar. His grin was really big, a reminder to smile at the customers.

Dutifully she showed her gritted teeth.

No surprise that by the time she started her second shift a headache beat behind her brown eyes. A gnawing low in her belly reminded her she hadn't eaten since leaving for the grocery store that morning. She'd meant to grab something at home, but she'd been running behind, and Tad's note had distracted her. Despite the hollow feeling, she lacked any desire for food.

She knew she should eat, to keep up her strength and

give her a dose of energy. Lately she'd allowed herself to become run-down. At least, that's all she'd thought her problem was until she realized she'd missed a period.

But she refused to think about the unlikely pregnancy right now. She blamed stress for her lack of appetite as she pushed the concept of a baby away along with the reminder to eat. The very notion of food made her queasy.

Which made serving the bar's specialty—greasy burgers and fries—no easy task. The combined scents of alcohol and sweat didn't help. Long before ten o'clock she regretted taking on the extra shift.

She'd be on until three, and the long, energy-sucking night stretched ahead of her. The Lord knew dodging the groping hands of randy sailors could be considered an aerobic sport.

"Jesse, order up."

Hoping to settle her stomach, she grabbed a sip of cola and went back to work.

Looking for a drink and some downtime, Navy Chief Brock Sullivan entered the Green Garter. Country rock boomed loud enough to prevent thought, and the savory tang of grilling meat and onions filled the air.

His stomach growled at the mouth-watering scent. Just what he needed.

In a glance he noted the presence of friends, trouble-makers and a brown-eyed, redheaded waitress. When it came to making the choice between the Garter and

Mac's Place on 31st, the view made the difference. Pretty and friendly, if a little young, the waitresses here had it all over Mac's Place.

Set to ship out in six days, he'd spent his duty hours drilling foreign procedure into his crew, including advising them on what was needed to put their personal effects in order for a stint overseas. He'd then spent four hours taking care of his own business.

"Brock," a voice hailed him from across the dim room.

He acknowledged the call with a wave but shook off the offer to join his fellow chiefs. Instead he chose to sit alone at his usual table in the corner.

He wanted a beer, a burger and an hour or two of bother-free time to himself.

Sprawled back in his chair, he watched the redhead approach. Call him a sexist, but he did admire a long-legged woman in a short black skirt. A white dress shirt, open to show a hint of cleavage, topped the skirt. A green garter worn high on her right thigh teased a man with the notion of peeling it from her body.

Too bad Jesse was too young for him, or he'd be tempted to spend a few hours of his remaining leave tangling the sheets with her. Seeing if her passion matched her fiery hair.

She reminded him of a time of youth and promise. Of another world and another woman, both lost to him long ago. Sherry rarely touched his thoughts after sixteen years, and when she did he lived with the guilt and her ghost for days.

"Evenin'," the redhead greeted in a husky, slightly weary tone. She blinked as if trying to bring him into focus. "What can I get you?"

One glance at her too-pale features immediately took his mind off the rest of her body. Something was wrong, real wrong. So white the pink on her cheeks and lips stood out in garish lines, she actively swayed on her feet.

"Hey." He instinctively reached out a hand, holding her steady with a hand under her elbow. "Are you okay?"

"I just need to sit." She licked dry lips, but he saw perspiration beaded her delicate brow. The hand clutching her order pad rested on her abdomen. "Dizzy."

"Sure. Here." He stood to help her. But before he got fully to his feet, her head wheeled and she crumpled into his arms. "Well hell."

"Jesse," an insistent, gentle voice called to her. "Jesse. Come back now."

Disoriented, she tried to place where she lay. The Green Garter, of course, but why was she on the floor? Why was her head spinning? What happened?

"Stand back, give her room. Jesse? Open those pretty brown eyes."

She recognized the voice but found it impossible to place. Forcing her eyes open, she looked directly into a light overhead. Flinching, she closed her eyes again, tried moving her head away from the glare. Cloth rustled under her. Someone had placed a jacket under her head, a jacket smelling of musk and man, the scent telling her exactly who stood over her attempting to revive her.

Brock Sullivan.

"That's my girl. Come on, sweetheart, open your eyes." The minty scent of toothpaste told her how close he was bent over her.

Too close. Soon he'd realize she was awake, and she'd have to open her eyes and face him.

Navy Chief Brock Sullivan. Always polite, always respectful, always the one the sailors went to in a crunch. A true gentleman, except for the hungry eyes.

Sometimes when he looked at her, she felt he wanted to eat her up.

More than once she'd thought if she weren't currently with Tad, she'd be tempted. Though Sullivan was over thirty, he was a fine specimen of manhood—over six feet, muscular but lean with it, and shoulders wide enough to carry the world.

She'd be crazy not to be tempted, especially when she looked into those true-blue eyes.

She'd heard the young crewmen talking about him. They always spoke of him with respect edged with fear. She got the impression he was strict but fair. He helped them out of tight spots but expected them to learn from their mistakes. And pay for them.

How embarrassing to fall flat at his feet. Maybe if she stayed very still, he and the others gathered around would leave her to expire of mortification on her own. Yeah, she thought as she listened to the advice being jockeyed back and forth, that was her best course of action. She had a good chance of the earth opening up and swallowing her whole. This was California after all.

Where was a good earthquake when you really needed it?

"She's not responding," another voice stated. "Time to call 911. She needs to go to the hospital."

No. She couldn't let them call 911. She had all of $39.80 in her bank account. She couldn't afford the cost of an ambulance or a hospital.

Forcing her eyes open, she looked right into Sullivan's vivid blue eyes.

She blinked once, twice.

"Hey," he greeted her in a voice both gentle and calm. "Welcome back. You were out for a couple of minutes. How do you feel?"

Because she saw real concern in the depths of those incredible eyes, she tried for a smile. "Peachy."

"Do you hurt anywhere?"

Hurt? Other than her pride? She took a minute to take stock. Her head throbbed, the nausea still churned her stomach and an ache beat on her left side below her waist. Too many sodas. So she'd cut back, switch to water and go back to work. "I'm fine. I missed lunch is all. I just got a little light-headed."

"Lunch, huh?" He quirked a dark brow. "It's ten o'clock. Does that mean you missed dinner, too?"

"Maybe." She frowned, disliking being caught in a weak moment. "I'm fine now."

To prove it, she tried to sit up. Immediately her head and stomach protested and the burn in her side flared again. Biting the inside of her lip, she tried to hide the hurt, continuing to move through the discomfort even as worry niggled at the back of her mind.

"Whoa, take it slow and easy." He instantly offered support, his hands warm and strong on her back and upper arm.

Weak and hurting, she leaned heavily on him as she climbed to her feet. The effort cost her in pain and strength. In pride. Gratefully she settled into the chair her manager pulled forward. Stan had hovered behind Sullivan the whole time he tended to her.

She realized Stan had been the one to suggest calling 911. Pulling her shoulders back, she sat up straighter to show everyone she was fine. She couldn't afford to be sick.

She focused on Stan. "I'm sorry for the trouble. I'm okay now. There's no need for the hospital."

As soon as the words left her mouth, black dots began to dance in front of her eyes. The same dots she'd seen before she fainted. Light-headed, she leaned forward in the chair letting her hair fall around her face to hide her condition from the men.

The black receded a bit, enough for her to feel the clamminess of her skin, the sweat breaking out on her brow.

No, not again. She fought off the dizziness, taking deep breaths. She needed to get back to work. She couldn't faint again.

A gentle yet insistent hand on her hair pushed her head down between her knees. Immediately she felt the blood flow back into her head. But the ache in her side intensified, and she clutched herself.

"Okay, that's it," Sullivan said. "I'm taking her to the emergency room."

"No," Jesse protested. She tried to sit up, but his hand in her hair kept her from raising her head. Her gaze fixed on the dirty tile floor, she argued against any need for medical attention. "It's just a headache." She tried to convince him as she had herself. "Some aspirin and a burger, I'll be fine."

She pushed against the weight of his hand and this time he let her up. Biting her lip at the discomfort in her side, she glared into his blue eyes.

"You have no right to manhandle me. I'm not going to the hospital, and you can't make me."

Her irritation bounced off him like bubbles off stone.

"Okay." He crossed his arms over his impressive chest. "Show me you can walk to the bar unassisted, and I'll leave you alone."

Jesse gauged the fifteen feet between her and the bar. Not so far. So she was a little light-headed. She'd still make it. She had no choice. She needed this job, which meant she had to make it to that bar.

Standing, more of a chore than usual, she caught her

balance. Beginning by placing one foot in front of the other, she took one step, then the next. Sullivan kept pace with her. She'd blast him with a killer look, but she couldn't spare the energy.

As Martina McBride proclaimed this one was for the girls, Jesse ran the gauntlet of eyes. The Green Garter catered to the Navy crowd. From ensigns to master chiefs, she had the attention of them all. This must have been what it felt like to walk the plank.

Except these men and women weren't her enemies. She felt their concern, their sympathy. Somehow that made it worse.

Swaying, she caught herself on a table, holding her side with the other hand. A young man jumped up to help her, grabbing her elbow to steady her. Frantically she shook her head, trying to pull away. She had to do it on her own.

Too late.

Sullivan moved in. He wrapped an arm around her waist and led her toward the door. "Lean on me."

His strength was too seductive to refuse. Knowing she'd fought as long and as hard as she dared, she accepted his support. Forcing down a burger wouldn't cure her problem.

"Wait," she pleaded when he led her outside to his black SUV, "I need my purse and coat."

Stan appeared a moment later with both items. "Is she going to be all right?"

"I'll let you know what the doctor says." Sullivan lifted her into the front seat.

Stan handed through her purse and coat. "You need me to call anybody for you?"

Thinking of Tad's goodbye note, she shook her head. He'd made it clear where he stood and it wasn't beside her.

She stole a glance at Sullivan's set profile. So strong, so sure, so confident he probably hadn't made a mistake in his entire life. How could he understand her life had been one mistake after another? That every day she struggled to hold everything together.

Yes, going to the hospital made sense. If she had the money to pay for medical treatment, which she didn't. Time for her to confess that truth to her companion.

She cleared her throat. "Listen, Chief…? Um, sir?" Exactly what did she call the man?

He glanced at her from the corners of his eyes. Looking back at the road, he held his right hand out toward her. "I'm Brock Sullivan. You can call me Brock."

CHAPTER TWO

BROCK. Right, okay, proper introductions were good.

"I'm Jesse." She placed her shaking hand in his. Immediate warmth and a gentle, steady grip enveloped her fingers.

"Nice to meet you, Jesse." He released her to return his hand to the wheel. "But if you're thinking of trying to talk me out of taking you to the hospital, save your breath."

"You could take me home. I'll be fine, I promise."

He shook his head. "Jesse, you passed out. People don't pass out for no reason. And you've been holding on to your side with a death grip. Something's wrong. I'm not leaving you alone until you've seen a doctor."

"I don't have the money, okay?" she blurted, shame curling in her belly. "I can't afford to pay the emergency room fees."

The matter-of-fact look he turned on her spoke volumes, questioning her worry of money over her health. "I'll cover the fees. You can pay me back."

He made it sound so easy, so reasonable. Which somehow made her feel worse. "I can't let you pay for me."

"Why not?"

Wonderful. Now he wanted her to explain her irrational feelings. Not easy to do when she didn't understand them herself.

All she knew, all that made it through the throbbing in her head, the rolling in her stomach, the pain that seemed to be everywhere, was it should be Tad with her.

And that truly was irrational. She'd received more compassion from this stranger in the past hour than she ever had from Tad.

Old habits died hard.

She'd only been in San Diego for a year, so she was by no means an authority on Navy etiquette, but she had learned one thing. A seaman's reputation mattered. The Navy supported family values and frowned heavily on sailors having their fun but not living up to their responsibilities.

Brock deserved to know what he was letting himself in for. Only fair she give him that consideration.

"I can't let you pay, because I think the doctor is going to tell me I'm pregnant."

The words hung heavy in the air between Brock and Jesse.

Even in profile she saw his brows rise, then settle into place. Otherwise he showed no reaction to her announcement except to say, "Then you can't afford not to see the doctor, can you?"

"I guess not." Jesse cringed down in her seat, hugging her middle. Fear and denial had been her constant companions since the first niggling suspicion of pregnancy had occurred to her.

Sure she wanted kids. Someday in the future. When she had a career, a husband, a home.

Now was not good.

Now was a no-future, no-benefits job, a deadbeat, former boyfriend and a cramped apartment with an unreliable roommate.

"I heard you tell Stan there was no one to call. Does that mean the father isn't in the picture?"

"Not anymore," she confirmed, no longer worried about her dignity. "He left me a goodbye letter this morning."

"Maybe if he knew—"

She raised a hand to stop him. "He taped the note to the home pregnancy test I bought last night. He found the test in my purse when he took my tip money."

"Scum."

She pursed her lips. "You're flattering him."

"So why were you with the guy?"

"Once upon a time, long, long ago, I loved him." She laughed wearily. "What's funny is I made the break. Moved all the way to San Diego to get rid of him."

He sent her a pointed look. "You must have gotten together at some point."

She closed her eyes and leaned her throbbing head against the soothing coolness of the glass window. Her left hand braced her on the seat. "He showed up a few months ago. Swore he'd changed. I held him off, but he really seemed different. He talked me into going to a party on Halloween. We were having a good time, drinking. It seemed like a good time to try again."

The silence struck her, and she opened her eyes to focus on his strong profile silhouetted by the lights from the dash. What was she thinking?

"I'm sorry," she told him, "TMI."

His gaze left the road to sweep over her. "TMI?"

"Too much information." She looked out her window, at the lights flashing by. "It was all a big mistake. And now I'm all alone." She trailed off to a whisper, more thought than spoken.

Who could blame her for ignoring all symptoms and the possibility of pregnancy for as long as possible? She'd become so good at pretending, she hadn't considered what her run-down condition meant to the baby. A new kind of fear cut like ice. She began to shudder as she prayed her ignorance and neglect hadn't harmed her baby.

His large, warm hand settled over hers on the seat. "You're not alone tonight."

He kept his promise. Brock never left Jesse alone. Not in the waiting room, not in the emergency room, not for a moment. Not until he was asked to step outside the cubicle while the doctor conducted his exam did Brock leave her side. Even then he only left after she indicated she'd be okay without him.

Dr. Wilcox, an older gentleman with white hair and a Vandyke beard, gently poked and probed, asked a few more questions, extremely personal questions she was happy Brock wasn't around to hear.

Of course, once a girl revealed she'd been left high and dry at her most vulnerable moment, she had few secrets left worth keeping. Answering when she last had a period, when she last engaged in intercourse were small potatoes after that.

Staring at the overhead light while the doctor completed his exam, Jesse bit off a humorless laugh. She'd already volunteered that last information to Brock.

Yeah, she was definitely on her stride today.

"You can sit up now," Dr. Wilcox told her. After explaining she was dehydrated, he had a nurse hook her up to an IV. He then called Brock back to join them.

"Ms. Manning, I can confirm you are pregnant."

The doctor continued to speak, but she didn't hear another word as her mind, her heart, her soul dealt with the reality of a child growing within her.

In a single instant love filled her to overflowing, full tears flooded her eyes and her hands, cradled over her child, began to shake. She forgot every moment of denial, regretted every harsh thought as joy and wonder replaced doubt and fear.

A sense of belonging, deeper than any she'd ever known, forged an unbreakable bond between her and her baby. Silently she vowed never to let her child down.

"Ms. Manning, are you listening?" Dr. Wilcox demanded.

Jesse blinked and focused on him. "Excuse me?"

Brock reached for her hand and squeezed. "You should start over, Doctor."

"You're going to have to take better care of yourself." His chastising look included Brock before the doctor turned his attention back to Jesse.

"As well as being dehydrated, you have a kidney infection, and your blood is low in iron. From what you tell me, you're just over two months along. Still in the first trimester, which is the most dangerous time for the fetus."

He leveled a stern gaze on Jesse that made her feel no bigger than a gnat and smaller still when he again moved the same stare to Brock who was innocent of any wrongdoing.

"You don't understand, Doctor—"

He held up a finger, stopping her explanation. "It's not up to me to understand, young lady. If you want to keep this baby, you need to make some changes. My recommendation is at least twenty-four hours' bed rest, followed by a month of light activity."

"A month..." Jesse whispered, appalled at the thought of the time off work.

"Get lots of rest, eat regular meals. I'm prescribing prenatal vitamins and iron. Drink lots of water. Cranberry juice is also good for kidney infection." He scribbled on a pad as he spoke, then handed her the paper.

"I want you to finish the IV, and I suggest you see an obstetrician soon."

He stood, tucked the pad and pen in his coat pocket. "Good luck, Ms. Manning." He shook her hand, nodded at Brock and left the cubicle.

Jesse pleated the paper, running her fingers over the crease again and again until Brock reached over and took it from her and placed it in her purse.

"Are you okay?" he asked.

She glanced up at him, aware she owed him an apology for the assumptions the doctor had made and the condemnation he'd shown Brock. He didn't deserve to be cast as the bad guy when he'd done nothing but help her.

She reached for his hand. Without hesitation he wrapped his larger hand around hers and lowered himself into the chair the doctor had vacated. Her fingers felt very small in Brock's grip, and it struck her again how strong and capable he was. She'd always be grateful to him for staying with her through this unreal night.

Forcing a smile for his benefit, she said, "Thank you so much for your help. Ever since I fainted everything has seemed surreal." She met his direct gaze, fearing contempt but finding only sympathy. "Just having you here, seeing a familiar face helped to keep me grounded."

"If having me here helped, I'm glad," he said simply.

"You'll never know how much." Torturing her lip

while uncertainty tortured her insides, she looked away. "I'm sorry the doctor blamed—"

"Stop right there." He squeezed her fingers. "You are not responsible for what the doctor thinks."

"But—"

"Jesse you can't take on every misinformed person out there. Life is too short for that kind of burden. Let it go."

"I'm still sorry. And I want you to know you don't have to stay here with me any longer."

He made no move to leave. "I'll stay to see you home."

Yes, please. She really didn't want to be in this cold, sterile place alone. Where the people were impersonal and judgmental. But the saline solution in the IV dripped slower than molasses, and she couldn't ask him to waste any more of his night on her. Especially when she saw the clock read 1:00 a.m.

"You've done enough. Besides I'm a big girl. I'll find my own way home."

He sat back in the chair, crossed his arms over his impressive chest and leveled a chief's stare on her. "How? Taking the bus?"

"No." She checked on the status of her drip, unable to look him in the eye as she lied. "A cab."

A gentle finger under her chin turned her back to him. "Don't start messing with me now, Jesse. No way are you paying for a cab when you're already worried about how you're going to take time off work for a month."

Embarrassment heated her skin at being caught. But that didn't mean he was obligated to stay.

A sweep of his thumb chased the red over her cheek, causing the heat to intensify. For a moment their gazes locked and held. Finally she lowered her eyes before she gave in to his persistence and begged him to stay.

"I'll be fine," she insisted.

He stood.

Instantly a flood of disappointment rushed through her. He was leaving. This time she couldn't even fake a smile.

She swallowed back tears. "Bye."

"I'm not going anywhere. Except the cafeteria. Would you like me to bring you something? You never got your burger."

Jesse stared at him, horrified. "Oh my God. All night you've been with me. You haven't eaten."

He winked at her. "It's not the first time. I'll survive. Will you be all right if I leave for a few minutes?"

"Of course."

"What would you like?"

Her stomach hadn't settled enough to like the thought of food. "Maybe some crackers if you can find some. And cranberry juice."

"Sure thing. Why don't you close your eyes and rest while I'm gone."

"I will." She nodded, though she didn't really want him to go.

She felt safe with him near, comforted by his concern. Without him the hospital was a cold, sterile place. But he would be out of her life soon enough; she needed to start getting used to the idea.

CHAPTER THREE

IT WAS nearly two when Brock helped Jesse to her door. He frowned as he surveyed the run-down condition of the apartment complex. Not surprising, considering the area.

More asleep than awake, Jesse stumbled. He moved his hand from her elbow to her waist to help her up the stairs to the second floor. The night had taken a toll on her, both emotionally and physically.

He felt the weight of fatigue himself after a twenty-hour day. And with his crew shipping out in a few days, he needed to be up and alert again in less than four hours.

Plus the sooner he delivered her into the safe haven of her home and got back to his life the better. She was a sweet kid—older than he'd originally thought but with twelve years between them, still a kid.

Music, loud in the early-morning stillness, beat behind the door Jesse stopped beside. A resigned look of disgust deepened the exhaustion on her face.

She blocked his path with a hand on his chest and tried for a smile no more successful than the pathetic attempts she'd made at the hospital. There wasn't a whole lot of pretense about Jesse.

"Thanks for all your help tonight." She hesitated as if wanting to say more, but she only opened the door and stepped inside. Behind her, smoke filled the room, thick and cloying. Three people, two men and a woman, sprawled across the mismatched furniture. Hip-hop came from a stereo on top of a plastic crate doing duty as a coffee table.

When the smoke hit Jesse, she went white then green.

With a bravery that told him of the effort it cost her, she lifted her chin and said goodbye.

"I won't forget what you did for me. Have a nice life."

Brock made it all the way back to the top of the stairs before his conscience got the better of him. Perhaps his memories of Sherry made him more sensitive tonight, but he couldn't leave Jesse to deal with that crowd alone.

If he'd listened to his gut and his brother sixteen years ago, he wouldn't have destroyed the most important things in his life. In one fell swoop he lost his fiancée, his future and his family's respect.

The thought of spending the next six months haunted by Jesse's courageous brown eyes turned Brock around. Determined strides carried him back to apartment 2B. He knocked, then stepped inside. The three in the living room looked at him with dazed disinterest.

"Hey, man." A limp young man with greasy brown hair roused enough to notice Brock. "You bring any with you?"

Brock ignored him, convinced he'd done the right thing in coming back for Jesse. He headed for the hall and the bedrooms figuring she'd go straight to bed. A movement to the left drew his attention. She sat at the kitchen table, her head in her hands.

She looked up when he stopped beside her. The fire of anger burned through the tears pooled in her whiskey-bright eyes. "Someone's in my bed."

He hunkered down to her level and ran a soothing hand over her thick amber hair. "Which room is yours?"

"The one on the right."

"Get your purse and jacket. I'll be right back." He pushed to his feet.

She grabbed his wrist. "Brock, it's okay."

He gently pried her fingers free and placed her hand on the table. "No, it's not. You'd better get what you need from the bathroom, as well. I'm taking you to my place for the night. I have an extra room in my condo. You can stay there."

In the hall, too grand a name for the four-foot-long space, he flipped open the door on the right and flicked on the lights. On the bed a man and woman sprang apart.

"Hey," the man yelped in outrage. "Get out. This room is occupied."

The woman grabbed the sheet to cover herself. The man yanked a pillow into his lap.

"Not anymore," Brock told him in the tone he reserved for raw recruits, sparing a glance for the woman. "Get dressed and get out. This room doesn't belong to you."

"Tracy said we could use it." The man muttered belligerently.

"Tracy doesn't pay the rent for this room. Jesse does. Do you have Jesse's permission to be here? No. So get dressed and leave. Now."

The couple glared at him, making no move to follow his directive. Brock put them from his mind. He went to the closet and pulled out a sport duffel. Going to the bureau, he filled the bag with the essentials he thought Jesse would need for the night.

He returned to the kitchen where she waited. She had her purse in her lap, her coat over her arm and a cosmetic bag on the table next to her.

"Ready?" he asked, reaching for her coat to help her into it.

Behind him the man and woman exited Jesse's room, went to the front door and left. Brock ignored them and the dark looks they sent his way.

Jesse watched them go, her total lack of expression telling him the extent of her weariness. "They're gone. I don't have to go now."

Funny, she didn't sound relieved. Then he saw her glance distastefully down the hall toward her room. Obviously, she found the thought of sleeping in a bed recently used for recreational purposes less than appealing.

It didn't matter. No way he was leaving her here.

"Can you walk or should I carry you?"

"You've already done too much," she protested. Pride showed in the lift of her chin even as tear-heavy brown eyes pleaded with him.

But pleaded for what? Did she want him to leave her alone or insist on her compliance? She sadly overestimated his stamina if she thought he had the ability, or patience, to read minds at this time of night.

"Jesse," a shrill voice called above the music. "Who is this guy? Where's Tad?"

Brock turned his attention to the living area where the washed-out blond woman perched on the edge of a brown plaid couch. He met her suspicious gaze impassively. Finally, a show of concern on Jesse's behalf. He'd begun to wonder if she had anyone who cared about her, who'd be there to help her through a difficult pregnancy.

Maybe she did just want him to leave.

"My roommate, Tracy," Jesse told him and then raised her voice to say, "Tad's gone."

The woman frowned. She reached out and turned off the stereo. Blessed silence followed.

"What did you say?" Her shrill attitude made him wish for the music back. "Where's Tad?"

"Gone," Jesse informed her flatly. "He left."

"Left where?" Tracy demanded. She licked her lips. "He usually brings the beer. Why are you home so early, anyway? I figured you'd taken a second shift."

So much for the roommate's concern.

"And what?" Jesse demanded. "You decided to throw a party?" The bite in the question didn't quite disguise the underlying disillusionment. "You told me this morning you were going to work a second shift to pay back the money you borrowed for the rent."

Tracy answered with a dismissive shrug. "There's plenty of time to make that up before rent is due again."

During all he'd seen her go through tonight, Jesse had lifted that delicate chin and kept on going. Now, for the first time, defeat stole the life from her expression.

He reached for her as her strength gave out and she went limp in his arms.

She looked up as if seeking reassurance from him. Then she blinked and the hope disappeared. "Please take me away from here."

That's all he needed to hear. He hooked the shoulder strap of her sport bag over his shoulder, then thrust her purse and cosmetic bag into her hands. But she stopped him when he would have swept her into his arms.

"I'm walking out of here on my own steam."

"Let's go." He nodded approval before he opened the door, and they were in the clean night air on the way home.

Jesse slept the day away. She'd been beyond thought, beyond emotion by the time Brock tucked her between the clean sheets of his spare bed.

"I have duty in a few hours." He'd competently and

impersonally helped her strip off her blouse, skirt and shoes. "Sleep as long as you want. Don't leave this bed except to use the bathroom and for meals. Help yourself to anything in the fridge. I'll be back around six."

She dragged the covers up to her chin. On principle she should protest his high-handed attitude, but sleeping for the next twelve hours sounded like heaven so she didn't.

A thought nagged at the back of her mind, and she finally came up with the memory of work.

"I have first shift tomorrow."

"The doctor said no work." He turned the switch on the bedside lamp until only the dim light in the base lit the room. "I'll call Stan in the morning and let him know you'll be out for two weeks."

She'd been going to protest—no way she could miss work—but the next thing she knew, she awoke to sunlight streaming around closed blinds.

She fought the waking, clinging to unconsciousness to combat the aches and pains waiting for her on the other side. Already the throbbing behind her eyeballs put a dent in her defenses.

In the end the need for the bathroom lost her the war.

Dragging her body out of bed, holding her tender head, she stumbled around until she found the navy-blue and pewter bathroom. Right where Brock Sullivan had told her it would be.

And it all came flowing back to her. The baby. Tad's leaving. The disaster at her place last night.

She didn't remember the part where she got hit by

the truck, the two-trailer semi, but it must have happened because that's what her body felt like.

The cool water felt so good against the skin of her hands, she splashed her face, too. And that felt wonderful, too. Then she remembered coming to, on the floor of the Green Garter, and the skanky feeling of strangers having sex in her bed. The mirror reflected the navy-blue shower curtain behind her. That's all the encouragement she needed to step out of her bra and panties and under the shower spray. For a few blessed moments she forgot everything else, even the memory of Brock stripping her of her clothes last night.

He'd truly seen her at her lowest. At least, she hoped it was her lowest.

What was she going to do? She had a baby growing inside her. She cupped her lower belly as the warm water ran over her. But the doctor said if she wanted to save the baby, she needed to rest and take it easy.

How was she going to take care of herself and the baby if she couldn't work?

By getting off her feet was the first answer, so she shut off the water, dried off, then wore the towel to the corner of the bedroom where Brock had thrown her bag. She searched through it twice, but he'd forgotten to include a nightie. The thought of tight jeans or shorts didn't appeal, so she pulled on clean panties and went in search of a T-shirt from Brock's room.

The gray carpeting in the hall moved right into his room. Black replaced the navy in here. Black, square-edged furniture topped the light-gray carpeting, while a pewter-gray comforter covered the bed he hadn't bothered to make this morning. Probably because he only got three hours of sleep last night.

The room smelled like him. Clean and masculine. It made her skin prickle. She'd been surrounded by that scent last night, and she was reminded of his strength and competency. She felt safe with him and cared for. And she wanted the feeling again.

So instead of searching for a clean shirt, she reached for the one tossed across a black chair. She held the white cotton to her nose and inhaled. Yes, that was his male scent. She pulled the shirt over her head and sighed. Better already.

Next she went to the kitchen where she took her vitamins with a full bottle of water. Then she drank a glass of cranberry juice that Brock had stopped for on their way to his place in the early hours of the morning.

Her energy gave out on her at that point, and she crashed back into bed.

"Excuse me, Chief. Do you have a minute, sir?"

Brock signed his authorization on a requisition, handed off the clipboard and turned his attention to the seaman apprentice waiting for a response. "What can I do for you, Sanchez?"

The young sailor glanced around nervously. Blood rose up his neck turning his swarthy complexion a ruddy brown. He cleared his throat, stretched his neck.

Brock's attention sharpened. "What is it, sailor? You have something to report?"

"No, sir." Another throat clearing. "Chief…sir, I was wondering…" He trailed off, took a deep breath, and grinned real big. "I'm getting married, sir, tomorrow. Would you be my best man, sir?"

Brock crossed his arms over his chest and fixed his concentration on his crewmember. Sea tours often provoked rushed marriages. In Brock's experience most such marriages failed to go the distance.

"Have you thought this through, Sanchez? Are you sure you don't want to wait until you get back? It's only a few months."

"No, man—I mean, no, sir." Sanchez didn't shuffle his feet, but Brock could tell it was a near thing. "I want to do this now. I love Angela. You made me see that when you made me question why I was always so jealous of her. I want to marry her." He lowered his voice. "She's pregnant. I want her to have good benefits, you know, while I'm gone."

For all his nervousness, Sanchez projected an aura of excitement. And he was stepping up, being responsible. Brock couldn't fault the young sailor for taking action like a man. Brock held out his hand.

"Congratulations. Sure I'll be your best man. Just tell me when and where."

Jesse woke up feeling human again. She was hungry, which she took as a good sign. Back in the kitchen she cut up an apple. Wanting a change of scenery from the bedroom, she carried her snack to the couch and put her feet up.

For the next hour and a half she tried to come up with a solution to her problem but still had no answers of how she could survive without working when Brock walked through the door at six.

Just seeing him lifted her spirits. A weird experience, one she'd truly never had before. Not at home, not with Tad. But here it was with this stranger at a time in her life when she needed it most.

Too bad it had to end so soon. No doubt he meant to take her home as soon as he got cleaned up. Not that he looked bad. He wore a beige uniform, short-sleeved with lots of bars on the arm. It gave him an aura of power and authority.

He came into the living room when he saw her and sat on the coffee table to survey her.

Self-conscious under his intense, blue scrutiny, she smiled shyly.

He nodded. "You're looking better. How do you feel?"

"Rested."

"That's good." He hit his thighs and rose to his feet. "I'm going to fix us some dinner, then we'll talk."

Talk? What did they have to talk about? She appreciated everything he'd done for her, but she wasn't his responsibility and she couldn't continue to allow him to take on her problems.

With that in mind she returned to the room he'd given her, made the bed and changed into her own clothes. She sat on the bed when she finished, amazed by how weak the slightest effort made her.

She hadn't called Stan today because Brock had said he would and because she didn't know what she was going to say when she finally talked to him. She knew she should consider alternatives to keeping her baby, not only for her sake but for the baby's, as well.

The love she already felt prevented her from exploring any other option. It may be selfish of her, but her heart demanded no other decision.

If that's what Brock meant to talk about, he could save his breath. She'd already made up her mind.

He grilled steaks, tossed a salad and baked potatoes. She ate a few bites of each, not managing more as she'd eaten the apple only a short while ago. She enjoyed watching him, the flex of muscle as he cut his meat, the strong movement of his jaw as he chewed, the focused concentration with which he did both.

He told her of his day, entertaining her with the comic antics of his crew as they got ready to ship out. She laughed, as he meant her to, but under the humor she grew saddened to hear he'd be leaving soon.

Oh no, she caught herself before the thought went any further. She had no business having feelings regarding him one way or another.

Hadn't she learned anything from Tad running out on her and their child? She should be cursing all men as scum. Look at the examples in her life. Her father had been a disinterested spectator, Tad a disinterested parasite, and tomorrow Stan would probably turn out to be a disinterested employer.

By no means prime specimens.

At the very least, she should mark Brock down in the disinterested stranger category and move on. She sighed. Okay, the incredibly gorgeous, disinterested stranger category.

So he'd been solicitous and gentle and attentive. So what?

So he'd gone out of his way for her not once, but twice. So what?

So he hadn't washed his hands of her when he could have. So what?

So he'd stripped her nearly bare without copping a feel. No big deal, right?

Wrong.

He'd been good to her when he didn't have to be. Better than anyone in a long, long time. She may not have known him for long, but yeah, she'd miss him when he left.

"You ready to talk?" Brock set a glass of cranberry juice on the coffee table within easy reach. He sat in the black leather La-Z-Boy adjacent to the couch.

"There's no reason to drag this out, Brock." She smiled to show no hard feelings. "I'm packed and ready to go."

"Not so fast. You shouldn't have to go through this pregnancy alone. Tell me more about Tad."

"Tad and I were best buddies since the fifth grade. My parents were undemonstrative people who should never have had a child. When he was lucky, Tad's parents flat-out ignored him. When he wasn't so lucky, he dodged fists and bottles. His dad had a hard time keeping a job, and his mother didn't even try. They got a divorce so she could claim welfare. It made me sick to hear her call her benefit installment a paycheck. They were the worst kind of parasites, always acting entitled as if the world owed them.

"I should have known Tad would turn out just like them."

"What about your family?" he asked.

She shook her head, emphatic in her response before he finished his question. "I was nothing more than a duty to my parents. I felt their indifference every day I lived in their home. I won't subject my child to the lack of emotion I grew up with." She swept her hair behind her ear. "We're better off on our own."

"You need to take it easy for the next six weeks. How are you going to manage that?"

Dread clenched her insides. Lord, she didn't know.

"The rent is paid for the next three weeks." She worked hard to keep the uncertainty out of her voice. "There must be some program to help me. I promised myself when things started getting bad, I'd never go on welfare. But my baby is more important than my pride. I'll do whatever is necessary to protect her."

"Her?"

Jesse frowned, confused by his question until she realized she'd given her baby a sex. A slip of the tongue there. But she couldn't deny wanting to give this child everything she hadn't had as a little girl. She may not have much in the way of creature comforts to offer, but she had overwhelming love. Which personal experience had taught her was the most precious gift a child could receive.

"Jesse, I have a suggestion." Brock leaned forward in the black chair. "I don't want you to answer right away. Take tonight, think about it. Tomorrow morning you can give me your answer, but no later, because I only have a few days. Whatever you decide, I want you to know you'll always be safe with me."

Dismayed, she met his gaze straight-on. Had he somehow read her negative thoughts? Looking into his clear, steady eyes, she saw his compassion, his honesty and knew she could trust him in ways she'd never been free to trust anyone before.

"You may think me a naive, trusting fool," she said. How could he not after she had so easily bared her entire awful history to him? "But don't worry about me. I can take care of myself. And I'll take care of my baby, too."

He lifted a hand toward her hair, but pulled back before touching her. "I think you're incredibly courageous and giving. And I don't think you should have to take care of yourself and the baby alone. I want to help. If you marry me, you'll have medical care and a place to stay."

She stared at him unblinking, truly uncomprehending for a full minute. "Marry you?"

"It's not as far-fetched as it sounds. The Navy provides full benefits. As my wife you'd have access to all of them. An obstetrician for you. A pediatrician for the baby. There'd be other Navy wives to help and advise you. You'd be able to take some classes, aim for a career."

Jesse blinked. It sounded wonderful.

In fact, it sounded too good to be true.

CHAPTER FOUR

JESSE propped an elbow on her knee and her chin on the heel of her hand. She eyed Brock as if he'd lost a few of his marbles.

"Why is it I'm the one that was dehydrated but you're the one that's delusional?"

The corner of his mouth quirked up. "It's a legitimate proposal. One of my sailors asked me to be his best man today. He decided to get married before he leaves so his wife will have his benefits. The conversation got me to thinking. If we got married, you'd have the medical care you need for yourself and the baby. I'll be gone, so you can stay here in the condo. I've got all the expenses covered on automatic payments."

She held up a hand to stop him. "Brock, I can't let you pay for me." She swallowed hard. "There must be a state program that helps women in my situation."

He reached for her hand. "I'd have to cover the expenses whether you lived here or not. You can take all the time you need to get back on your feet, then go back to work, go to school, take a trade course, whatever you want."

Lord, his offer sounded heavenly.

Anyone else and she'd worry about a sexual price tag being attached to the proposition. But this was simply Sullivan helping out in a crunch. It's what he did. That knowledge didn't keep her pride from rebelling, but her pragmatic side demanded she see the advantages.

Could she do it? Marry a stranger?

Damn straight, if it meant saving her child.

His offer meant she could take her time recuperating, then find a job with better hours where she wasn't constantly on her feet. And with no rent to pay maybe she could pursue her education. She'd always dreamed of being a kindergarten teacher and had been saving up to take classes before Tad had cleaned her out.

Tears welled up at the thought of going back to school. It was something she'd wanted for so long.

"Jesse." Brock squeezed her fingers. "What do you think? Will you marry me?"

Jesse blinked away the tears, bringing his handsome features into focus. Nobody had ever done as much for her as he had, and yet here he was offering to do so much more.

Okay, time for a reality check. Such an important decision deserved more than ten minutes' deliberation.

She reached out to cup his cheek, felt the bristles from his five-o'clock shadow. She met his blue eyes straight-on. "Thank you so much for that beautiful proposal. You said I could take tonight to think about it?"

"Of course." He covered her hand with his, his warmth enveloping her. Was it her imagination that he lingered over the caress before releasing her? "You can't take long though. I leave in five days. I'll take you home. Or would you like to stay here tonight?"

Because she very much would, she shook her head. "Thank you, but I need to go home."

He nodded and stood. "Will you be rested enough to go with me to the ceremony tomorrow?"

"I've slept the entire day away. And I confess I feel better. The doctor said twenty-four hours. So, yes, I'd like to go with you."

"Good. You can give me your answer then. And if you agree, we can get married right away."

Jesse sat on her bed and looked at her watch for the fourth time in two minutes. Another ten minutes before Brock would arrive to pick her up.

And she wouldn't be coming back.

A half hour after walking through the door last night she'd made up her mind to accept his proposal.

At the foot of the bed all her possessions filled a suitcase, a sport duffel bag and two boxes. Not much to represent twenty-three years of existence. She reminded herself she got rid of a lot of stuff when she decided to move to California.

And life wasn't about things, anyway.

So what did it say about her that she'd found more joy in her few possessions than in the people in her life?

After being harassed by Tracy within minutes of returning yesterday, Jesse took it to mean she needed to hang with a better quality of people. Responsible people. People with honor and morals. People who cared for each other, who did things for each other without thought of the return.

People like Brock Sullivan.

For her baby's sake, Jesse would accept the opportunity he offered her. And somehow, someday she'd find a way to repay him.

The doorbell sounded, sending her heartbeat skidding. She jumped to her feet, took a deep breath and wiped damp palms on the seat of her denim skirt. Time to greet her future.

Lord, she hoped he hadn't changed his mind. Surely, he'd have called if he had.

Unless he was too much of a man to let her down over the phone. Her pulse spiked as the truth of that thought registered.

"Stop being a wuss," she admonished herself. "Brock's not an indecisive, immature boy. He's a man who knows his own mind. He wouldn't have proposed if he didn't mean it."

The pep talk got her to the door. And the sight that met her took her breath away.

Decked out in dress blues, Brock stood straight and proud. Even standing at ease, the formal Navy uniform enhanced his air of command, his natural confidence. Tall and broad-shouldered, eyes sharp, smart and deep blue, he looked cool, assured and slightly dangerous.

Oh, my. The spike in her pulse this time had nothing to do with dread and everything to do with wanting the military man standing before her. She suddenly understood the appeal of a man in uniform.

"Hi." She licked her lips and smiled.

"Hello," he drawled, returning her smile. He inclined his head. "You ready to go?"

"Ready?" she repeated, distracted by his sexy grin.

One dark eyebrow lifted, and amusement lightened his eyes as he crossed the threshold. "For the wedding?"

"The wedding, right." Flushing, she shook off the daze his presence had triggered. "I'm ready." She cleared her throat, gauging his expression, trying to determine if he regretted his offer to marry her. She inhaled, then let the breath out slowly. "And I'm packed. Unless you've changed your mind about helping me out?"

"I don't change my mind," he said with a confidence she envied. "We'll be at the county building. If you're truly decided, we can get married today."

She blinked and her heart kick-started into overdrive. Wow, that was fast, but then he'd said they didn't have much time with him leaving so soon. Was she truly decided? Thinking of the alternative—a run-down apartment with an unsympathetic parasite of a roommate, and a go-nowhere, no-benefits job that she probably didn't even have anymore—caused her frantic heartbeat to calm.

"Oh, yeah. I'm sure." She started for the hall. "My things are in my room."

He caught her arm. "I'll get your stuff."

"It's not much but more than you can carry. I can get one of the boxes. It's not too heavy."

"I'll make two trips. You're not carrying anything." He handed her his keys. "Open the back of the SUV for me. I'm parked on the street."

He disappeared into her old room, and she headed outside. Walking down the stairs, she glanced down at her black boots, black denim miniskirt and lightweight, pink sweater. Not exactly what she'd have chosen to get married in. She sighed and looked on the bright side. It was better than jeans and a T-shirt, her usual attire.

She reached the car and opened the back just as he walked up behind her. He'd managed to get everything in one trip after all, by stacking the boxes on top of the suitcase. She admired both his ingenuity and his strength.

"Wow, my muscle man." Better to tease him than get stuck on her lack of possessions again, or worse have him focus on it.

He winked as he placed his load down. "I work out."

She eyed the wide expanse of his chest decorated with Navy symbols. "I bet you do."

The light breeze shifted, blowing her hair across her eyes. She flipped her head into the wind, hoping the strands would fall away. They didn't.

"Let me." Brock gently swept the wayward lock of hair aside, his fingers trailing heat across her cheek.

"Thank you." Jesse turned away from his gentleness, from the heat. When she reached for the door handle, he beat her, opening the door and helping her into her seat. So thoughtful, so much the gentleman. She forced a smile as she buckled up.

She couldn't afford to be attracted to him. He'd be her husband, yet her yearning for him was not only misplaced, it was inappropriate.

His motives for offering to help her remained a mystery, but she recognized his strong sense of duty, of responsibility at work. She'd grown up bathed in the cold indifference of obligation. She'd accepted Brock's proposal for the baby's sake, otherwise she'd never put herself in an apathetic relationship again.

Sanchez, his pretty bride, Angela, and twenty of their family members filled the small county clerk's office to overflowing. The room buzzed with excitement, laughter and emotional bursts of tears.

The demonstration of family love struck Brock as overwhelming and distressingly familiar. Long ago he'd known the benefits of family support; in the past sixteen years he'd learned to live without it.

While the young couple filled out the paperwork for their marriage license, Brock led Jesse to a cubicle where they completed their own paperwork.

Though she participated fully in the process and

offered no objection to performing the ceremony following the Sanchez wedding, Brock had seen the way she'd given herself the once-over earlier. He may not be the most sensitive man on the planet, but he understood a woman's wedding day should be special.

He excused himself, and put in a call to his friend Jake who agreed to stand as his best man. Brock then put in a call to Jake's wife, Emily. When he returned to the cubicle, he announced a change.

"We won't be able to do this now after all," he told Jesse. "I have to get back to the base. Can you recommend a justice of the peace for an evening ceremony?" he asked the clerk.

The young woman stood. "Let me see if anyone here can help you. What time were you thinking?"

"Five-thirty, out on the lawn." Brock looked to Jesse for confirmation and she nodded. "Do you mind killing a few hours at Horton Plaza?"

Jesse's gaze followed the woman, then switched to him. "Sure. But we don't have to do this today if it's not convenient."

The clerk returned to advise them a justice of the peace was available to marry them that evening.

Brock thanked the woman. "Today is good," he assured Jesse. "We're just busy with the cruise pending."

"Sir." Sanchez appeared at the opening of the cubicle. A huge smile lit his features. "We're ready."

"Then let's get you married, sailor." Brock stood and

held out his hand to her. "Before that beautiful bride of yours comes to her senses."

Sanchez laughed. "Yes, sir."

Jesse pressed close to Brock as they moved around the partition to join the wedding party. "It's nice of you to do this for him."

He made a sound of acknowledgment that sounded a lot like a grunt.

Because of the beautiful day and large assembly, Angela and Sanchez chose to have the ceremony outside. Her hand clasped in Brock's, Jesse followed the procession down the stairs and outside to the lawn. A leafy, sprawling tree provided a lush background for the ceremony.

She would have held back, but Brock pulled her up front with him. Not by word or action had he indicated any level of unease. He stood tall and proud—head and shoulders above everyone else—and chatted with several members of the wedding party, in Spanish no less, even complimenting both mothers on their appearance and the wise choice their child had made.

Only his unrelenting grip on her hand spoke of his gratitude for her presence. It made him a little more human. Sometimes he was too good to be true.

"He thinks highly of you," she whispered to Brock. It showed in the respectful way Sanchez addressed Brock. And in the fact that with all the family available, Sanchez had chosen his chief to stand up with him.

"He's a good kid."

"They make a sweet couple. Very much in love."

Sanchez, splendid in his dress uniform, held the petite Angela by the waist. He clearly adored the woman he planned to share his life with.

"It'll take more than love for them to make it. Marriage to a sailor takes strength and sacrifice. She's pregnant and he's leaving on a six-month cruise. It won't be easy for either of them."

The similarities in their situations struck Jesse. It told her a lot about Brock, because from his tone he gave their marriage of convenience a better chance than the marriage of love. She looked at the happy crowd, the smiles and hugs being exchanged and she knew better.

"They'll make it."

"Oh, yeah?" He slanted her an amused look. "What makes you so sure?"

"Their families." Her heart recognized exactly why Sanchez and Angela would make it because it was everything she'd ever dreamed of. Unconditional love. "The love and support here, the examples of successful relationships will help them through the hard times."

"Right." The edge in his voice drew Jesse's gaze back to him. All signs of amusement were gone. "They're ready to start."

The ceremony flew by; soon Brock was shaking Sanchez's hand and kissing the bride.

Jesse stepped forward to offer her own best wishes.

"*Gracias.*" Angela beamed at Jesse. "You are to marry today, also?" She looked at Brock then rolled her eyes suggestively. "You are a lucky woman. Chief Sullivan is the best of men. *¿Y muy guapo, verdad?* Very handsome." She laughed and kissed Jesse's cheek. "Good luck to you."

Jesse, who acknowledged a new appreciation for men in uniform, nodded. "I'm very lucky."

Jesse expected Brock to drop her off at Horton Plaza, a multilevel maze of a mall located less than a mile from the county building in downtown San Diego. With over a hundred shops, including a movie theater, she'd be able to while away hours simply window-shopping.

The idea of shopping for a wedding dress tempted her, but with little more than thirty dollars in her purse she couldn't afford the luxury. She tried to pretend it didn't sting, that a business arrangement didn't require a special dress. Unfortunately the self-deception didn't work.

Brock pulled into the parking garage. Surprised, she turned to him. "I thought you were just going to drop me off."

"I have a few minutes." He swung the SUV into a parking slot. "I want to make sure you're okay before I leave."

Figuring that meant making sure she ate, Jesse fell into step with him. She could eat. She hadn't had much appetite earlier waiting for him to arrive, worrying if he'd changed him mind.

When he turned left and entered Nordstrom, she

began to realize she needed to stop making assumptions when it came to him.

She came to a dead stop right by a display of Gucci handbags. "Brock, why are we here?"

He continued on a few steps before he realized she wasn't meekly following his lead. Unfazed by her hesitation or her question, he backtracked, wrapped a hard arm around her waist and urged her forward.

"No arguing." He cut off further questions. "I have it on good authority this is the place to go for brides-to-be."

"Brock, no." Jesse dragged her feet, a futile gesture with his easy strength sweeping her along. Being distracted by the heat of his touch didn't help. "I don't know what you have planned, but it's not necessary. You're already doing more than enough."

Winning by virtue of refusing to respond, Brock led her into customer service where he requested the services of a personal shopper.

The gentleman behind the counter made a phone call and then advised Brock, "Diana will be right with you."

"Thank you." Jesse offered the man a wide smile. "Will you excuse us for a moment. Darling, I really must talk to you." Determined not to be railroaded, Jesse looped her arm around Brock's elbow and drew him aside. "I can't afford this place."

"Jesse." He lifted her hand from his arm to his mouth and kissed her fingers. "I want to do this for you."

"Stop that." She yanked her hand away, knowing by the gleam in his eyes that he was playing to their audience just as she had. "I don't want you spending money on me. Accepting benefits and living in a house you're already paying for is one thing. Buying clothes is another. I don't need anything. I don't want anything."

"Too bad. This is my gift to you."

"No."

"Yes."

"Why?"

He sighed, obviously unused to being challenged. "Can't you just be gracious and accept the gift?"

"Not unless you tell me why." She crossed her arms over her chest and lifted her chin. Best he learn early in their relationship that, contrary to her compliance so far, she had a mind and will of her own. "I'm already in your debt."

"Okay." Glancing around, he shifted, putting his back to the counter and moving her further into the corner of the service lobby. "Our marriage may be for expedience, but our marriage license isn't just a contract."

"What do you mean?" That's exactly how Jesse saw it, although she was definitely on the receiving end of the benefits.

"I mean a marriage has meaning and purpose. And we may be rushed, but adding some pomp and ceremony to the wedding will remind us of the importance of it going forward."

"Mr. Sullivan." A tall brunette in a flowing skirt topped with a fitted jacket approached them. "I'm Diana, your personal shopper."

While Brock greeted the woman and asked her to give them a few minutes, Jesse considered what he'd said. He spoke the truth. They were entering into more than a contract. So how did she feel about that? Was he suddenly wanting more out of the arrangement?

As soon as she had his attention again, she grabbed his arm and walked him out of the customer service area into the bedding department.

"Jesse, are you okay?"

"What's changed? What do you want?" Jesse demanded.

He frowned. "What are you talking about? Nothing's changed."

"You said our marriage is more than a contract. What do you want? Because I'm not going to prostitute myself for medical benefits."

His head snapped back as if she'd hit him. But he recovered quickly, squaring his shoulders, narrowing blue eyes icier than she'd ever seen them.

"If you believe that, we can end this right here, right now."

"I've offended you."

"Yes." He didn't bother denying the obvious.

"Well, I'm sorry." And she was, because he'd done so much for her, offered so much. Yet at what cost? "But I need to know what I'm getting myself into."

"We discussed this."

"Let's discuss it again. What's the pomp and ceremony supposed to put me in mind of?"

"Being my wife. The wife of Chief Brock Sullivan. You'll be responsible for my reputation while I'm gone. You'll be interacting with other Navy wives, families. What you do will reflect on me."

"And you're afraid I'll tarnish your pretty name?" Now she felt the bite of insult.

"Not really, no. If I'd thought that, I never would have proposed. But I need you to be aware of it and a proper ceremony with all the frills will act as a good reminder. So do me a favor and get your hair done, your nails, whatever women do for special occasions. You're supposed to be taking it easy, anyway. This will give you a chance to relax."

She rocked back on her heels then forward. He had a valid point, a genuine concern, and she felt small for not trusting him.

Would it be so hard for her to do this for him? Hadn't she watched the Sanchez wedding with a touch of envy? Hadn't she longed for a better dress for the occasion? It burned her pride to accept more from Brock. Still, how could she refuse the first thing he'd asked of her?

"Okay," she finally agreed. "But just so you know, it's not possible for a bride to relax on her wedding day. It's against the law of nature."

He shook his head, tucked that masterful arm around her one more time and walked her into customer service. "Jesse, you're nothing if not contrary. If anyone can manage it, it's you."

CHAPTER FIVE

"WITH the power vested in me by the state of California, I now pronounce you husband and wife. You may kiss the bride."

The justice of the peace beamed on Jesse and Brock as the woman uttered the words that joined their lives. For Jesse it was one powerhouse statement followed by another.

Husband and wife. And the groom was expected to kiss the bride.

Standing close to Brock, in the finery he'd insisted she needed, holding the bouquet of fresh white roses he'd surprised her with, Jesse realized she'd been waiting for this moment. She wanted his mouth on hers, those strong arms enfolding her, pulling her close.

For a moment the familiar flare of hunger heated his eyes, and she knew he shared her longing, but when he bent toward her he aimed for her cheek.

Oh, no. She wouldn't be cheated; this may be her only chance to know his touch, his taste.

Time for the bride to kiss the groom.

Going up on her toes, she met him halfway and, cupping his cheek, directed his mouth to hers. For a millisecond he stilled, and fear ratcheted through her that this perfect instant under the brilliant fading sun would end in mortifying rejection. Witnessed by Brock's friends, the justice of the peace and her assistant.

Then his control broke. He claimed her mouth, stealing all coherent thought, leaving only sensation. The soft demand of his lips, the sweep and thrust of his tongue sent her blood pressure soaring. She nestled into his embrace, savoring the steely strength of his solid chest, the firmness of his muscular arms.

Both generous and masterful, he took over the kiss, bending over her to deepen his possession, making her feel cherished and sexy, an intoxicating combination.

"Ah-hum."

The sound of a throat clearing made a dent in Jesse's lust-induced haze. She tightened her arms around Brock's neck, holding him in place, not wanting the moment to end.

More disciplined, Brock lifted his head, but she didn't let him go without a fight. She caught his lower lip between her teeth. With a low groan he sank back into the kiss, sipping from her lips twice, three times before setting her aside and stepping back.

"Ah-hum. Step aside, old man." Jake Reed, Brock's best friend, a bald Denzel Washington look-alike, deftly insinuated himself between Jesse and her new husband. "It's time for the best man to kiss the bride."

Wary, she looked up into laughing brown eyes. Jake winked, but the devilry in his expression made her wonder if she should be reassured or take cover. His gentle kiss on the cheek eased her mind.

"And I'm a great believer in equal rights. The matron of honor gets to kiss the groom, too." Emily Reed, a lovely woman with mocha skin and lush curves sidled up to Brock and crooked her finger at him to bend down. "Come here, handsome."

With a grin Brock complied, causing the woman to giggle by dipping her over his arm and giving her a quick kiss on the mouth.

Jesse understood exactly why Emily came up fanning herself. Brock knew how to handle a woman. She found she didn't care for the thought of his hands on another woman. Not that Jesse had any business thinking of him in those terms.

To distract herself she turned to the justice of the peace and her assistant to express appreciation for the women staying late to accommodate the evening wedding.

"It was our pleasure, dear," the justice assured Jesse. "This is the best part of the job."

"Tell her about your record, Elsa," the assistant urged. "A bride deserves good news on her wedding day."

Good news, what a refreshing idea.

"Yes, please share," Jesse invited.

"It's nothing too dramatic. I just have a talent for

guessing which marriages will last. I don't usually like to say anything, but I was telling Lydia the two of you have what it takes. I can see it in the way you look at each other."

How ironic. Of all the things the woman could say, that was the last thing Jesse expected to hear.

How they looked at each other, huh? She respected and admired him, no big surprise considering he'd treated her better than anyone in a long time. Plus he was *muy guapo,* very handsome. So she knew what her gaze revealed.

But what, Jesse wondered, did Elsa see in Brock's gaze?

And did it matter when not only would they not make it for the long term, their plan was for the short term?

"She's a beautiful girl." Jake came to stand by Brock and followed his gaze to where Jesse spoke with the justice of the peace. "Do you know what the hell you're doing?"

Brock faced his friend. "I know you must be surprised."

"You think?" Jake shook his head, concern and puzzlement in his gaze. "How many times have I heard you lecture the sailors not to marry in haste? And here you are with someone you barely know. And she's just a kid."

"I'm beginning to realize she was never a kid."

Brock's gaze returned to Jesse. The evening breeze flirted with the hem of her dress, lifting it to show a length of shapely thigh decorated with a green garter. He smiled at the sentimentality. "And I've learned it's not the quantity of time you spend with someone, it's the quality."

"So you love her?" Jake cut to the chase as Emily joined them.

"I care about her." Brock couldn't lie to his best friends. "She's smart and brave and has a huge heart."

"Brock—" Emily began.

"And she's pregnant."

"Oh."

"I know what I'm doing," Brock assured them. "It means a lot to me that you care, that you stood up with me today. Emily, I'm hoping you'll take her under your wing while I'm gone."

Emily looked from Brock to Jesse and back. "You know I'm a sucker for a happy ending." She rose onto her toes to kiss his cheek. "You can count on me."

Emily and Jake insisted on treating Jesse and Brock to a wedding dinner. After initial protests, Brock gave in to the suggestion and agreed to follow the couple to a popular seafood restaurant with a harbor view.

In the car Jesse leaned back in her seat and closed her eyes. She couldn't believe how tired she felt. All she really wanted to do was go home and go to bed.

Her eyes popped opened when she realized her exhaustion didn't prevent her picturing her new husband beside her in bed. Beside her, over her, inside her. Oh, my.

From the corner of her eye she admired his strong profile dimly highlighted by the dash lights. Now she knew how he tasted, how it felt to be wanted by him, she longed for more time in his arms.

But that would be a huge mistake. On so many levels. She knew she trusted too easily and it got her into trouble sometimes, but this time was different. This time she didn't want to mess it up.

"I know you're tired." Brock's voice rescued her from her thoughts. He reached for her hand and gave it a squeeze. "We won't stay long. I promise. Jake and Emily dropped everything to help me—us—out today. I didn't want to disappoint them."

"I'm fine," she assured him. "Just sleepy, which is ridiculous. I mean, all I've done today is shop, pamper myself and attend two weddings. Nothing strenuous there."

"You moved out of your home today, got married and you're pregnant." He pulled into a parking space and set the SUV in gear before turning his amused gaze on her. "You're right, no stress there."

She grinned. "Well, when you put it like that."

"That's better." He lifted his hand as if to touch her, but at the last instant detoured to gently tug on a curling tendril of hair. "You look beautiful."

"Thank you." Emotion caused the words to come out

husky. She cleared her throat and made a show of running her finger along the row of ribbons on his chest. "You look pretty sharp yourself. I was proud to stand beside you today."

"Jesse." He shook his head. "I don't know what to say to that."

"You don't need to say anything. I just wanted you to know I appreciate everything you've done for me." She ran her knuckles along the wool lapel of his navy jacket. "And that you looked good doing it."

"Jesse," he said again, caution in his deep voice. "We shouldn't—"

"No, no. I know," she assured him. "This isn't about getting together. Not that I'm not tempted, because—" Oh, God had she just said that? "Never mind. What I'm trying to say is your reputation is safe with me."

Holding her gaze, he nodded and then his smile flashed white in the dim interior. "Thank you."

Finally the time came when Jesse stood dockside waiting to say goodbye to Brock. Dampness hung heavy in the early-morning air. He'd told her not to bother for his sake, he'd had many deployments with no send-off. Which of course motivated her even more to make the effort.

Shivering, she danced from foot to foot to generate warmth while she searched the somber crowd of couples and families for her errant husband. As soon as they'd arrived, one of his sailors had dragged Brock off to oversee something.

He'd warned her they'd only have a few minutes before he went onboard ship and that the dock would be sheer chaos, but she insisted on getting out of the car and she intended to stay until the ship left.

A proper goodbye was all she had to give him; she meant to do it right.

"Sorry about that." Brock appeared at her side. "Are you okay?" He made no move to touch her in any of the million small ways he usually did.

Surprising, because she'd known him for such a small amount of time, how she missed the sense of connection those casual touches gave her. She understood he'd begun to distance himself to make it easier to leave. Hadn't she used the trick a time or two herself?

"I'm good. No need to worry about me. I'm not here to be entertained. You do what you have to do."

"I really have to get onboard." He glanced at the crowd, at the ship, at his watch.

He looked anywhere and everywhere but at her. And she couldn't take her eyes off him. Maybe she'd been wrong to come here. She hadn't meant to make this harder on him.

"You should go, then." She summoned a smile to ease the moment. "I know you have people waiting."

Finally his gaze focused on her. "But you're not going to leave." He made it a statement.

"No," she confirmed. "I'm going to wait to wave goodbye."

He looked away, then back at her. "You don't need

to stay. I'm going to be busy. I won't be able to come out to the rail."

"Yeah, I figured." She eliminated some of the distance he'd created by moving a step closer to him. "But you'll know I'm here, wishing you farewell. Praying you come back safe and sound."

"Jesse." The flash of emotion in his eyes almost undid her. The distance disappeared completely when he cupped the back of her neck and laid his forehead on hers. "No one's ever—"

He didn't finish. He didn't need to. And it hurt to think of such a strong, giving man being so alone.

"Shh." Eyes closed, she lifted and angled her head until her lips brushed his. He immediately claimed her mouth in a torrid kiss.

She sank into the power of his embrace, desperate to assuage the need that had grown through the close proximity of the past few days.

They'd been in each other's pockets as he prepared to leave. Every little action ratcheted up the awareness another degree. Sitting side by side as he went over the finances and taught her how to use his computer, she'd been enticed by the smell of him, man and soap and a hint of spice. A simple ride up the coast as he assured himself she could handle the SUV became a session in torment as they blew through the romantic, moonlit night.

Oh, yeah, this is what she'd craved. His mouth on hers, demanding, claiming, savoring. Satisfying the sweet tension of being near but not touching, of being up close but impersonal. She roped her arms around his neck and snuggled flush against his body, branding the memory of him on her very psyche.

The pull of his arms drawing her closer, demanding her compliance revealed his surrender to the awareness between them.

No, not surrender, that was too tame a description. An erupting volcano would be a better description. Like lava flowing, when his control blew, the blaze of his passion consumed everything in its path.

His hand slid inside her jacket, found the swell of her breast and squeezed. She caught her breath, sensitive from pregnancy, his touch bordering on being too much. For all his fierceness, he immediately gentled his hold. Her nipples drew taut, pushing through lace and cotton to press into the palm of his hand.

His tongue invaded, persuaded, delighted. Who needed to breathe when pleasure tingled through her body from her painted toenails to her sparking synapses? Sensation stole all sense of time and place until the growing crowd jostled them, nearly knocking Jesse out of Brock's arms.

Lifting his head, he caught her to him, putting his back to the intrusion. "Damn crush."

She had to blink him into focus. Her heightened senses taking a moment to settle enough for her to see.

"Whew!" She blew out a breath and tested the strength of her knees. "Hold me or I'm going down."

He muffled a laugh, the rumble of his chest vibrating under her cheek. "Sweetheart, I have the opposite problem. We can stand here as long as you need."

She felt his problem pressed against her hip and smiled. Which was probably not the nicest reaction, but she liked that he wanted her. And she liked to hear him laugh—something he did so rarely—especially today. She hated to think of him leaving time after time with no one to see him off. How lonely that must have been.

She knew loneliness, and Brock deserved better.

Looking into his face, she wondered how she could ever have thought of him as old. Solid and strong, yes; experienced and caring, yes; hot, oh, yeah; old, she'd never make that mistake again.

Jeez, good thing he was leaving or she'd be in a world of trouble.

"I'm going to miss you," she whispered, unsure if she wanted him to hear.

He responded by running his hand down the length of her hair. "You can e-mail me anytime. I want to hear what the doctor says at your next appointment."

"Oh, that'll be exciting." She drew back and adjusted her jacket. "Hearing about my iron level and how I should keep my weight up or down."

"It's all part of the experience." He tugged a curl then brushed her hands away to fasten the button of her jacket, a totally unnecessary action as the dew-heavy morning had turned balmy for her. "Just be sure to take care of yourself."

"I will. And you have to promise to be careful."

"Always. I've got to go."

"No." She cupped his cheek and made him look at her. "Don't just say the words, you have to mean them. Promise me."

"Jesse, I'm a highly trained chief in the Navy, I can take care of myself."

"See that you do." She rose onto her toes for one last kiss. "I'll be waiting right here."

CHAPTER SIX

FROM: grngartergirl@airnet.com
Sent: January 31, 2:15 p.m.
To: chfsullivan@navy.mil
Subject: farewell to arms

Brock,

This morning was the most meaningful time of my life. The emotion of the crowd, the bravery of the departing sailors, the majesty of the ship, the whole experience overwhelmed me.

It was both humbling and exhilarating seeing our servicemen standing proud at the rail of the ship. Hundreds of men and women leaving behind all they love to serve the nation. I was honored to be there.

And I realize, you know, that you're still taking care of me even though you're already gone. Emily joined me after you left, and I know you arranged for her to find me. It's okay though. This is Jake's third deployment since they got married. I think she needed me more than I needed her, so you did good. We cried together and became fast friends. She offered to go to my doctor's appointment with me. For moral support. How cool is that?

I've never had a close woman friend before. I think I'm going to like it.

You don't need to worry about me, you know. I haven't been at my best since we met, but I assure you I've been taking care of myself for a long time and I'm going to be just fine. And because of you, my baby's going to be just fine, too. I will find a way to repay you for all that you've done to help my baby and me.

To start I'll be writing you every day. Yeah, yeah, that's not what you signed on for. Don't worry about it. You don't have to respond. This is just my gift to you, a connection to home while you're gone.

Regards,

Jesse

P.S. I think I saw you at the rail. Don't correct me if I'm wrong. It's one of my favorite memories.

From: chfsullivan@navy.mil
Sent: January 31, 10:23 p.m.
To: grngartergirl@airnet.com
Subject: farewell to arms

Jesse,

The honor is ours. I'm glad you and Emily are hitting it off.

Brock

P.S. Mine too.

From: grngartergirl@airnet.com
Sent: February 6, 1:28 p.m.
To: chfsullivan@navy.mil
Subject: doctor appointment

Brock,

Good news! The doctor gave me a clean bill of health. I'm to get plenty of rest, keep up my vitamins and do moderate exercise. He says the baby has a strong heartbeat and he plans to do an ultrasound in a couple of months.

They can tell you the sex at that point, but I'm not sure if I want to know. I've already got it in my mind this is a girl. I guess I should find out for sure so I can make the adjustment to boy if necessary.

I don't really care either way as long as the baby is healthy. It's a cliché, I know, but so true. I can't tell you how much I love this baby, or how far I'd go to protect it.

Snap! Who am I talking to? You know exactly the lengths I'll go to for the baby.

Now I have the doctor's release, I plan to start working again. Emily told me of an opening at the base preschool, which is perfect, as someday I want to be a teacher. I can't continue to let you support me. I won't make as much as I did at the bar, but thanks to you, I don't need to. And I want to take some classes. I won't overdo it, but I want to get as much done as possible before the baby is born.

Regards,
Jesse

From: grngartergirl@airnet.com
Sent: March 28, 11:52 p.m.
To: chfsullivan@navy.mil
Subject: baby moves
Brock,
The most amazing thing happened today. I felt the smallest of little flutters in my belly. At first I was concerned but then I realized it was a miracle. The baby moved.
I just needed to tell someone, and I thought of you. My baby is alive and growing and moving.
You should see my belly. I'm huge. I can no longer see my feet or button my jeans. Tomorrow I'm going to buy my first pair of maternity pants.
Oh, gosh, I'm crying. You should be happy you're not here. I cry at the least little thing. Good or bad, happy or sad, doesn't matter. Emily just pats my back and hands me a tissue.
I have to go. I have a test tomorrow, which I'm going to ace. I love my classes and working at the preschool. I'm going to make a great kindergarten teacher.
Oh, there it is again. The baby moved. Just there, do you feel it? I put the mouse right over the movement. I wish you were here to share this moment.
Until tomorrow,
Jesse

From: chfsullivan@navy.mil
Sent: March 29, 6:40 a.m.
To: grngartergirl@airnet.com

Subject: baby moves

Jesse,

You described the movements so vividly, I swear I did feel the baby moving. I can only imagine the wonder you must feel.

I needed to hear some good news. My day wasn't so good. One of my sailors had an accident and nearly lost a limb. Thank God the surgeon was able to save the arm. I spent most of the day making arrangements for the sailor to be flown home.

Some say he's the lucky one.

Today, I agree. I'd much rather be there celebrating with you than sending a broken man home to his family. I have no doubt you did ace the test. You've worked hard enough.

Take care of mom and baby.

Brock

From: grngartergirl@airnet.com
Sent: April 9, 6:29 p.m.
To: chfsullivan@navy.mil
Subject: baby news

Brock,

It's a girl!

I'm so happy. Excited. Ecstatic. And so tired. I'm falling asleep on my feet. But I needed to tell you first thing. I've included an attachment of the ultrasound. It's a girl! Sweet, sweet, sweet.

Did I mention how excited I am?

Cheers,

Jesse

From: chfsullivan@navy.mil
Sent: April 10, 6:40 a.m.
To: grngartergirl@airnet.com
Subject: baby news
Jesse,
Why are you surprised? You knew from the very beginning it was a girl. You should trust yourself more. You have good instincts. Especially where people are concerned. The article you sent on positive reinforcement gave me some ideas for improving morale here on ship. Worked too.
I'm glad you have your girl. Congratulations.
Brock

From: grngartergirl@airnet.com
Sent: May 16, 4:07 p.m.
To: chfsullivan@navy.mil
Subject: I'm a bad person
Oh Brock,
I wish you were here to put your strong arms around me. I need the peace and sense of safety I feel when you're near. You helped me through the lowest moments in my life. Even at the hospital hearing I'd put my baby at risk by denying the probable rather than taking responsibility for my actions, you gave me a sense of direction, of hope for the future.
Tad came to the condo today. Tracy gave him my address. He apologized for skipping out on me, said he wanted to do his part for the baby, that he intended to be a part of her life.
God, Brock, he was so high his words slurred. Then

he asked for money to help get on his feet so he could be there for his baby.

So I lied.

Don't be mad, but I told him the baby was yours. I told him we'd been together before he came back, that my night with him was a mistake. And I asked him to leave.

I'm not sorry either. I refuse to be sorry.

He left me. Knowing I may be pregnant, he left and stole from me on his way out the door. He stuck his goodbye note on the pregnancy test to make sure I got the point. Well, I did. He wanted no part of his daughter then, and I'm going to grant him that wish now.

I refuse to let him get his hooks into her. She's not even born and he's using her to get money for drugs. Some might say he has the right to know the baby is his. I say he had his chance.

I bought his "I'm going to change" story too many times to fall for it now. He's not the boy I knew and loved. I can't make the mistake of believing in him again. Not when my daughter would be the one to suffer.

I'm sorry I used you. You've been so good to me and I just keep taking and taking.

I'm not a good person. But I'm going to be an exceptional mother.

Jesse—ashamed but resolute

From: chfsullivan@navy.mil
Sent: May 16, 8:00 p.m.
To: grngartergirl@airnet.com

Subject: don't be stupid

I can't believe you're beating yourself up over this guy. He's a loser. Forget him. If I were there, my fist would be rocking his teeth. I'd teach him not to mess with my girls.

Brock—on his way to the gym to beat something up

P.S. If it gives you peace of mind, put my name on the birth certificate.

From: grngartergirl@airnet.com
Sent: May 16, 10:10 p.m.
To: chfsullivan@navy.mil
Subject: Overreaction

You crazy man,

Talk about unbelievable. There was no need to send your SEAL buddies over here to check on me. You'll be happy to know they checked all the locks, both windows and doors, and I've been secured for the night.

Honestly, Tad's never hurt me physically and I doubt he ever would. Then again drugs change people. So I guess I'm glad to know I'm safe. And that the country's most elite fighting force will occasionally be checking up on me.

Jesse—shaking her head in wonder

From: chfsullivan@navy.mil
Sent: June 5, 6:40 a.m.
To: grngartergirl@airnet.com
Subject: Itinerary update

Jesse,
We heard today that our deployment has been extended by two months. I'm sorry I won't be there for the birth of the baby. I'll keep you posted on updates.
Brock

Jesse fought through a medicated cloud of fuzzy inertia. Something waited for her on the other side, something precious. She couldn't quite remember what, but she wanted to get there, needed to get there to see.

She opened her eyes to a sterile room of pale green, the intermittent beeping of monitors and a tall man with a buzz cut holding a tiny, pink, wrapped bundle against his wide chest.

Brock. Here.

And he looked fine in jeans and a beige cotton T-shirt that hugged the defined muscles in the strong arms holding her baby.

Her baby. Something precious indeed.

How she wished Brock really were here, that any minute he'd walk over and place her baby in her arms. That would be the sweetest moment of all.

Too bad it was just a dream.

He wasn't here. And her baby was never going to be born. She had this dream all the time only to wake up alone and huge.

Of course the fuzziness was new. And the underlying discomfort that threatened real pain if she moved too much.

She blinked, then watched the imaginary Brock bend his head to kiss the fantasy baby's cheek.

"I want one of those," she told him. May as well play out the whole dream.

Brock turned. "You're awake." He moved to the side of the bed and stood over her gently rocking the baby. "So what do you want, the baby or a kiss?"

"Both." She grinned. Hey, it was her dream, she could have it all in her make-believe world. Reaching out, she snagged a belt loop on his jeans and drew him closer. "The kiss first."

"Whatever Mama wants." Careful of the baby, he bent over her. "Mama gets." The familiar scent of soap, spice and Brock added a layer of reality generally missing from her fantasies. But it was the touch of his mouth to hers, the soft claiming of lips both sweet and hungry that jolted her to reality.

"Oh God," she said against his mouth, "you're real."

He truly was here.

Tears rushed to her eyes. Somehow a miracle happened while she slept. Her baby had been born. And Brock had appeared from half a world away.

"My baby." Emotion choked her so the words barely reached a whisper.

"Allie's right here." He placed the pink bundle in her arms. "She's as beautiful as her mother."

The tears overflowed as memory returned. The planned Cesarean. How she'd tried so hard not to reveal her disappointment to Brock that he wouldn't be here for Allie's birth. How afraid she'd been going into the operation, anxious for her daughter to be born but scared of the unknown, of the surgery, of raising a child alone.

She remembered now hearing Emily calling out as they wheeled her away that Brock was coming. Half out of it, Jesse hadn't completely understood, but she hadn't been afraid anymore, either.

Now, holding the tiny being that belonged to her, opening the blanket to count fingers and toes, she experienced a new level of awe, even if Allie did sleep through the whole examination. "She's beautiful."

"Prettiest baby in the hospital," Brock agreed. "She takes after her mama." He tucked a burnished red curl behind her ear. "How are you doing?"

"My baby's here." She flashed him a half-shy glance. "You're here. I've never been better."

"Not quite what I meant." He grinned and settled on the side of the bed.

"Nothing else is important," she assured him. Her fingers lightly traced the curve of Allie's tiny features, the fluff of red-gold curls. "How is it possible you're here? You're supposed to be in the Persian Gulf."

He shrugged. "When you wrote that the doctor wanted to do a Cesarean birth I started making plans. I had leave coming so I hitched a ride on a supply plane and pulled in a few favors to snag a couple of West-bound flights and here I am."

She reached for his hand. "I'm so glad."

"Me too." He brought her fingers to his lips for a soft kiss. "I can't stay long. I have to leave by eight Monday night."

"So soon?" Only three days. Jesse heard the disappointment in her voice and cringed. He'd come all this way for her. A tear escaped to slide down her cheek. She swiped it away. The last thing she wanted was for him to regret making the effort. "I'm sorry. Pay no attention to me."

"Hey, we'll make the most of the time we have. As for the rest, you just had a baby. You're allowed to be emotional. Cut yourself some slack."

"You're so good to me." She licked dry lips, and he immediately handed her a cup of water from the bedside tray. "You always seem to know exactly what I need at any given moment." Next came a tissue, and she glanced at him through her lashes. "It's almost scary."

He cocked his head. "You're kidding me, right? You allow me to do so little for you. Listen, there's something I have to tell you—"

Just then a baby's cry announced little Allie wanted attention.

"Ah, Mama's little girl is awake. Mama's miracle." Jesse cooed as she lifted Allie against her chest. The baby turned her head in a seeking motion as she sucked on her miniature fist.

Brock watched mother and child, not bothering to turn away when Jesse opened her gown to bring Allie to her breast. The poignant sight of the newborn nursing reached right to his gut.

This, exactly this, was why he served in the Navy. To protect the peace of moments like this, which everyone should be able to enjoy.

For whatever inexplicable reason, he'd felt connected to Allie since he'd been at Jesse's side in the hospital when the doctor confirmed her pregnancy. He had no rights, no obligations, which was how he usually preferred it.

But not this time. God help him, he had to fight instincts to set up a college fund.

Jesse looked up at him, her face full of wonder, inviting him to share in the special moment. He reached down to tenderly stroke the baby's cheek as she suckled from her mother's breast.

He'd never been more moved or aroused in his life.

So, he'd restrain himself from planning Allie's future, but he could make sure she—and her mother— continued to have a safe place to live.

She'd interrupted him before he could tell Jesse his news. One reason he'd made this impromptu trip was to tell her of his promotion.

It was a great opportunity. Added another ribbon to his sleeve. And would keep him out of the country for another eight months.

That might just be enough time for him to get his cool perspective back.

CHAPTER SEVEN

JUST under six months later, Jesse struggled through the front door, baby carrier hooked around one arm, three bags of groceries around the other.

The phone began to ring before she could put either down. She set both on the table and reached for the cordless receiver on the island.

"Hello." Tucking the phone between chin and shoulder, she went to work releasing Allie from the carrier.

"Is this Jesse Sullivan?" an officious male voice queried. "Mrs. Brock Sullivan?"

"Yes." Jesse tensed. This didn't sound good. Had something happened to Brock? "Who's calling please?"

"This is Officer Thomlinson with Navy Fleet Command. I'm sorry to tell you there was an accident onboard—"

Jesse's knees gave out on her at the word *accident* and her head began to spin. She sank into a dining room chair.

"Wait. I'm sorry, can you please repeat that?"

"Chief Sullivan was injured in an accident onboard

ship. They stabilized him there then he was airlifted to Germany where they performed surgery."

"What kind of surgery? What are his injuries?" Jesse found it hard to breathe. "Is he okay?"

"His leg was broken in several places during a storm when a cable broke. He suffered some internal injuries. Chief Sullivan pushed two sailors aside and took the brunt of the falling equipment. He came through surgery well and is scheduled to return to San Diego tomorrow. He'll be taken to Balboa Hospital. You can see him there after 9:00 p.m."

Jesse gathered her wits and grabbed a pen and paper to take down the details. Her insides were cold as ice. Brock always seemed bigger than life, strong and sturdy. He was her rock.

He lived and worked on an aircraft carrier stationed in the Persian Gulf. Of course she knew he faced risks. But he always played them down, and she allowed the illusion because it kept the worry and fear at bay.

Twenty-six hours stretched in front of her. She wasn't sure how she'd fill the time, but she did know one thing for certain. She'd be there for Brock in any way he needed her.

The stillness kept Brock awake; even with his eyes closed and the pain medicated into the background, the lack of movement prevented him from pretending he was back on ship. Or that the events of the past seventy-two hours were anything more than a bad dream.

No, the nightmare was all too real.

The beige walls, curtainless windows, incessant beeping and stink of antiseptic recalled the lowest days of his life. He'd prayed never to see the inside of a hospital again.

No such luck.

In an instant he'd lost everything: his career, his future, the use of his left leg. Hell, he'd almost lost the leg altogether.

Oh, they were spouting optimistic drivel: the operation went well, the prognosis was good, with time and physical therapy he'd be good as new.

Bull.

He'd sent enough broken men home to know the drill. Keep the spirits up, offer hope. Never let them see concern or pity, when all you could think was "Poor bastard," as you shipped them back to their families.

Family. Yeah, this was how he wanted to come home. Jesse already had a six-month-old to feed, bathe and clothe. She needed help, not another person to feed, bathe and clothe. Especially not a grown man and one she was accustomed to receiving aid from not giving to.

He hated, *hated* that he was returning to her a crushed and broken man.

Why was it he never managed to come through for the people in his life? He always found a way to let them down.

"Hey, bro." A deep male voice spoke from the

shadows near the door. "I hear you manufactured a little accident to gain an early return."

Emotion swamped Brock, joy, sadness, love, pain, connection, loss: a confusing mix that compounded his miserable mood.

"Hell, it's barely a scratch. I don't know why everyone is overreacting." He pushed the lever to lift the head of the bed. Pain crackled through bone and muscle sending a firestorm up his left leg. He clenched his teeth and ignored it.

He wouldn't have this conversation lying flat on his back. Gathering all his strength, he prepared to bluff his way through a conversation with his baby brother.

The man flipped on the light and moved further into the room. His assessing blue gaze rolled over Brock, missing nothing, certainly not the pain he fought to hide.

"That's the Navy for you, always overreacting, sending good men home." Ford Sullivan slid into the single visitor's chair, kicked his feet out in front of him and crossed his hands over his stomach. "It's a wonder they have anyone left manning the ships."

"Shut up." Brock dismissed his youngest brother's sarcastic humor. "How'd you know I was here?" Also in the Navy, Ford tended to show up whenever they were in the same part of the world at the same time. The visits were both a blessing and a curse. "I haven't been back in San Diego more than a couple of hours."

"I have my sources. And they're very, very good."

"You wrote me you were out of the SEALs." As a

member of the Navy's elite special forces, Ford had traveled the world on clandestine missions unapproachable by larger forces. Until two months ago, he'd had access to intelligence few people ever saw, and then he transferred to a position as a SEAL trainer.

Obviously, he still had his feelers out for any Intel on Brock. But what the hell, Brock had his feelers out for Intel on Ford, too.

Just because Brock lost his place in the family, didn't mean he didn't care.

"Once a SEAL always a SEAL," Ford claimed with well-deserved arrogance. He indicated Brock's leg with a nod of his head. "So what's the prognosis?"

"They did reconstructive surgery, added a pin or two. They say the surgery went well but they won't be able to state anything with certainty until the cast comes off."

"That's good, then."

"Yeah." Unless the surgery didn't take, then it would be bye-bye Navy, but Brock kept that news to himself.

Not that Ford didn't know. He'd participated in too many high-risk missions not to know what the result of injuries meant to a sailor's career.

"Listen, Brock." Ford sat forward, his expression turning earnest. "You're going to need help while you're out of commission. Why don't you come home. You know Gram would love to have you."

Brock froze. "I don't think that's a good idea. Besides, I have help."

"Damn it, Brock. Don't you think you've punished yourself long enough?"

"I don't know what you're talking about. I'm not punishing anyone."

"Sherry's death wasn't your fault. It was an accident."

"I was driving. Whose fault was it if it wasn't mine?"

"It was Sherry who insisted on leaving, even though fog blanketed the roads. It was an accident," Ford repeated, his tone emphatic. "That means it was no one's fault. It's time to forgive yourself and put the past behind you. Come home, we miss you."

"My decision, my responsibility. I believe that's how Alex put it." The pain of that denouncement still hurt after eighteen years. As the oldest of six boys, at fourteen and twelve the two of them had joined forces to help raise their younger brothers after their parents died in a car accident in South America.

He and Alex had been a team; they'd covered each other's backs.

When Alex went off on Brock after the accident, it destroyed him. Shaken and bruised, Sherry dead because of him, he'd been woefully unprepared to handle his older brother's wrath and disappointment.

Ford's hand on his arm brought Brock back to the moment.

"Look, I don't know what happened between you and Alex back then," Ford said, "but you should know he misses you more than anyone."

Wallowing in the past made Brock's head hurt, or maybe it was trying to think through the heavy meds. "How could you know that?"

"I've watched him over the past eighteen years. I can tell you it meant the world to him when you showed up to be his best man in Las Vegas. We thought we'd hear from you, see more of you. After that it was a disappointment to all of us when that didn't happen. But Alex took it hard. For a happy man, he was miserable."

Brock shook his head. "I can't think about this now."

"There's nothing to think about. Just know we want you to come home."

"Have you told anyone I'm here, or about the accident?"

Ford sighed. "No."

"Good. Give me some time will you?" Brock let his head fall back on the pillow. "I need to be on my feet and thinking straight before I face the family."

"You're making this harder than it needs to be. We love you, Brock. It's that simple."

"I'm 38, Ford. I was twenty when I left home. You said it yourself, I haven't been around much in the past eighteen years. You hardly know me."

Ford laughed. "I was around for the all-important formative years. Bro, I know you plenty."

Brock conjured up a vision of a scrawny ten-year-old struggling to keep up with the big boys, and succeeding most of the time. SEAL training had just been more of the same for Ford.

Weary and feverish, he just wanted the conversation over. "You've given me a lot to think about."

"Good." Unselfconsciously, Ford carefully pulled Brock into a one-armed hug. "Take what time you need. But I'm warning you, I can't lie to Gram. You have until she next asks me how you're doing before you have a whole lot of family landing on your doorstep." Ford moved to the door. "Do yourself a favor, come to your senses and come home."

Jesse's footsteps echoed down the hospital corridor as she looked for Room 414. Most of the rooms were dark because of the late hour. She experienced a moment of doubt. Maybe she should have waited until the morning to come. No. She shook off the uncertainty. She needed to see Brock, to assure herself he was truly safe and all in one piece.

And he needed to see a friendly face, to know someone cared about what happened to him.

She picked up her pace, anxious to find him. She turned a corner and almost ran into a tall dark-haired man.

"Excuse me." The man smiled and stepped around her.

"Sure." Jesse looked after the man, something about him striking her as familiar. Then she realized he reminded her of Brock, similar build, similar coloring.

Thoughts of the man slipped away when she spotted Room 414 up ahead. Light spilled into the hall from the open door. Brock was up.

Her heart began to race. How ridiculous to be nervous. She'd shared so much with him through e-mail, letters and the occasional phone call that she felt she'd exposed her soul to him and learned about him in return. Yet person-to-person they were practically strangers.

No wimping out now, she squared her shoulders and stepped into the light.

Brock sat propped up in bed, naked from the waist up, his skin, tanned a golden brown, contrasted sharply with the stark white of his sheets and the thigh-high cast encasing his left leg. When Jesse got closer, she saw bruises and contusions over his left shoulder and down his arm.

Despite the light, his eyes were closed. Even in repose his features were drawn and a frown marred the smooth line of his brows. It didn't appear to be a restful slumber.

She moved to the bedside and lightly touched his hand. "Brock."

His eyes instantly opened, the same vivid blue she remembered so well but lacking the alert intensity she'd come to associate with him. It broke Jesse's heart to see such a strong man brought so low.

"Jesse." His hand turned over and his fingers tangled with hers. "You shouldn't have come out so late."

"You're home. You're hurt. Of course I came." She instantly wrapped his hand in hers. "How do you feel?"

He just shook his head. "I'm not going to be good company."

"I don't expect you to be." She sank into the chair next to the bed. "You don't have to entertain me."

"Where's Allie?"

"I dropped her at Emily's. She's going to keep her for the night. And don't tell me I don't need to stay, because I'm not leaving." Maybe she shouldn't have come. Maybe he didn't want her here.

The corner of his mouth curled up in a half smile. "Stubborn."

"You bet." She relaxed slightly. He wasn't his usual self, and he shouldn't have to be. And really, she needed to stop worrying about herself and focus on him. "Tell me what the doctors say."

The question stole all his animation. "They were happy with the results of the surgery, but because of the torn tendons and muscles, they're not sure if the leg will ever be as strong as it was. They had to put a couple of pins in the shin. I have six to eight weeks in the cast, then physical therapy."

"Brock, you're healthy and strong and stubborn as they come. You'll overcome this." Jesse wrapped his hand in both of hers. The flat delivery obviously hid a wealth of worry and pain. "How long do you have to stay in here?"

"Hopefully just overnight." He closed his eyes and shifted restlessly. "Which is still one night too many."

He looked so uncomfortable Jesse suggested, "Why don't you put the bed down and rest?"

When he didn't argue, she helped him get settled,

fluffed his pillows and arranged them to his satisfaction. He didn't speak again but fell into a fitful sleep.

After a while Jesse slipped away to find someone who would give her more details on his condition. She could feel the heat of fever radiating from him. Which indicated infection of some kind.

He wouldn't be content to stay hospitalized for long. Which suited her fine. She wanted him home where she could take proper care of him.

She just needed to find someone to tell her what that entailed.

Brock knew when Jesse left. And when she returned. He always knew when she was near.

Always. Hell. As if they'd actually spent any time together.

Didn't seem to matter. In the few days they'd been in each other's company, his body tuned itself to hers and it went on alert anytime she entered his vicinity. He might even have done something about it, too, except he'd torn himself up.

He was probably fooling himself anyway, to think she'd be interested in him simply because she shared herself so openly while he was gone. Didn't he warn his sailors against the illusion of Internet communication? How the disembodied connection allowed for a false sense of intimacy.

The Lord knew he'd told Jesse more than he ever intended to over the past fourteen months.

The nurses came, did their poking and prodding, changed his IV and went. He ignored them. Except to ask if they had a more comfortable chair for Jesse to use.

They brought in a narrow recliner, and Jesse curled on her side facing him. She didn't chitchat, which he appreciated—he wasn't up for a lot of conversation—but not once did she let go of his hand.

The warmth and softness of her grip grounded him when the painkillers blurred his edges, the night stretched on forever and the nurses disturbed the little sleep he managed to get. She'd given up the comfort of her bed and the care of her child to stay by his side.

He wouldn't have asked it of her, but he was glad she was here with him.

As seven o'clock rolled around and the early-morning sun filled the room highlighting Jesse's red hair into a blaze of glory, he watched her sleep and made up his mind. No matter what the doctors said, today he was going home.

Never had his condo represented peace, security and solace more than it did right now. And it had nothing to do with the fact it was home and everything to do with Jesse.

And that scared him more than any bad news the doctors could give him.

CHAPTER EIGHT

THAT afternoon the sound of the doorbell sent twin feelings of relief and anticipation zipping through Jesse. Spiced with just a pinch of anxiety.

No doubt this was Emily and Jake bringing Allie home. This would be the first time Brock saw Allie except for his brief visit when she'd been mere hours old. What would he think of her precious little girl?

Jesse quickly rinsed and dried her hands before heading for the door. On the way she cast a glance at Brock seated in the leather recliner. He appeared to be asleep, but she knew better. One moment he lounged with eyes closed, head to the side, the next she'd check on him to find him watching her.

She gently shook his arm as she passed. "The Reeds are here."

"Right." He shifted, flinched, then scrubbed a hand over his face. "I'm awake."

He'd been somber and restless ever since they got home around two. Unlike this morning; he'd been a firecracker at the hospital, demanding to be released when the doctors obviously preferred to keep him under observation for another day.

Navy doctors were used to getting their own way. But one thing she'd learned about Brock—he had an iron will of his own. She'd asked him once what he did in the Navy. He said he worked in air traffic control, and it was his job to make sure things happened how and when they were supposed to happen. Without fail.

Yeah, the man had a real talent for making things happen, so to nobody's surprise he soon had a release from medical custody. He'd have to go back as an outpatient every day until the doctors were satisfied, but he'd be sleeping in his own bed tonight.

The bed she usually slept in.

Bother. Why'd she have to think of that now? The visual of him in her bed as she'd seen him in the hospital yesterday, half-naked, all golden skin and hard muscles with the sheet pooled at his waist, sent heat rushing through her, causing her cheeks to be inordinately pink when she reached the door.

No help for it. She blew out a sigh, pasted on a smile and opened the door.

"Emily, Jake. Come in." Jesse stepped aside for them to enter, catching her bundle of love as she launched herself from Emily's arms. "Hello, sweet pea." She cuddled Allie close and met Emily's lively brown gaze. "Thanks for watching Allie."

"Oh, pooh." Emily waved the words away. "She's a

doll. Slept right through the night. Besides," she said, patting her rounded belly, "I needed the practice."

"You won't convince me of that." Jesse bounced Allie on her hip. "You're the best mother I know."

"Next to you maybe." Emily's attention turned to Brock. "How is he?"

"Stubborn. I know it was important to him to be home, but I almost wish he'd stayed one more night in the hospital. Much as he pretends otherwise, only pride and sheer force of will are keeping him upright in that chair. And his fever worries me."

"Honey, for a man who's been away as long as he has, who's been through what he's been through, there is no better medicine than being home. He just needs some good loving and he'll be fine."

Jesse chewed her lip and hitched Allie higher on her hip. "You think so?"

"I know so. And we won't stay long, I promise." She turned to follow Jake deeper into the room.

The men shook hands and then Jake stood awkwardly next to the leather recliner as if uncomfortable with being whole and hearty while his friend was laid low.

Emily showed no such hesitation; she bustled forward and, careful of his injury, bent to kiss Brock's cheek. "How's the patient?"

"Better now you're here, beautiful." Brock flashed a weak version of his killer smile.

"Uh-huh. Nothing wrong with your vision." She flapped her hands at Jake, herding him ahead of her to the sofa. "I'm so glad you're home safe and sound. Jake says you could have been crushed."

Brock's gaze slashed to Jesse before returning to Emily. "An exaggeration."

"Oh, God." Jesse sank into an armchair as her knees went weak. She hugged Allie against her. How close had she come to losing him?

"Good job, Em." Jake frowned his displeasure at his wife. "Now you've upset Jesse."

"Oh, hell no." Emily ruffled up like a riled hen protecting her chick. "Don't tell me the big strong men are trying to save the little women from life's harsh reality. Spare me, please." She jumped up, her ire propelling her around the room. "The *truth* doesn't upset us. Not knowing upsets us. Lies upset us. Pretending everything is all right when it's not upsets us."

"Emily, it's okay." Jesse tried to calm her friend, to get the visit back on track. She'd deal with Brock later.

"It's not okay." Emily waved her hands in the air, palms out. "We know what you do, the dangers involved. We handle it because we have to, because we love you, because we're Navy wives and we're tough. Don't you dare treat us like some namby-pamby girls. We're women. We can handle the truth."

A stunned silence followed her impassioned speech. Brock and Jake both looked shell-shocked.

"Eeeh." Allie burbled, breaking the tension, then she clapped her little hands together and grinned at Emily.

"Amen." Jesse joined the girls in their bid for

honesty. Jesse and Brock's marriage might not be conventional, but she'd always thought they had a special openness and candor that held them together. "The truth and nothing but the truth."

"Yeah, mama." Emily grinned, then just as fast as she riled up she switched gears again. She bent and lifted Allie into her arms. "Don't you think it's time this little girl met her daddy?"

Jesse felt her smile waver. Oh. How would Brock feel about being called daddy? He always showed an interest in Allie, asked after her, sent her presents from distant ports, encouraged Jesse to send pictures, even talked to her on the phone.

But this was different. This was claiming her as his in front of his closest friends. Would he choose now to tell them the truth?

Neither she nor Brock had talked much about the end of their relationship. There'd been no need as he hadn't been due to return for another couple of months. But now he was here, and so far they'd been making it up as they went along.

"About time." Brock immediately reached for Allie, putting Jesse's initial worries to rest. "In another minute I was going to get up and go to her."

"That would be something to see." Emily laughed and handed Allie to Brock.

He lowered the baby into his lap and fluffed her pretty pink dress around her. "Aren't you pretty as a doll. Did you get all dressed up for me?"

Okay, good start. Now to see if the two got along.

He talked gently to Allie, not baby talk, man to girl talk. Jesse's little girl, with her burgundy curls and big brown eyes, sucked on two fingers and studied him intently.

"Have you been taking care of your mama, like we discussed?" He didn't rush her, which was good. He let her come to him. "And remember, no boys until you're at least thirty."

Allie watched and listened, her tiny body tense, unsure if she liked the situation. Whether she liked him.

Until Brock flashed his smile. As usual, the crooked charm of his grin hit Jesse square in the gut. And Allie proved she was her mother's daughter. She gave him a huge, one-toothed grin and launched herself against his chest, laying her head on his shoulder.

Tears sprang to Jesse's eyes. He looked so big, so strong holding the tiny, fragile baby, and both were so close to her heart. Seeing them together touched her in ways she never imagined.

"I'll get us something to drink." Needing a moment alone, she hopped up and escaped to the kitchen, which was no real escape as it opened onto the dining-living area. She grabbed a handful of paper towels and turned on the cold water. Once she had a compress, she backed into the corner, pressed the cool wad to her eyes and allowed the tears to flow.

An arm came around her shoulders accompanied by the scent of White Shoulders, Emily's favorite perfume.

"Go ahead and cry. Your man is home. A little bent, but that'll mend. He's safe, that's what counts. And you have a beautiful baby together. If that's not worth a few tears, I don't know what is."

"I j-just want them to l-like each other." Jesse mopped her eyes.

"Girlfriend, it was love at first sight for both of them." ·

"I know." Jesse drew in a shuddering breath, trying for calm. "That's why I'm crying."

"No. You can forget it. Maybe tomorrow night."

"I want it tonight. Are you going to help me with the protection or not?"

"Not." Jesse stood arms akimbo in front of Brock, blocking him from the bathroom. "You're running a low-grade fever and you're weaving on your feet. No way I'm letting you take a shower. You'll fall on your butt."

"Then it'll be a clean butt. Step aside." Brock crowded closer, forcing her right up against the door. His eyes were a little glazed from the fever, and the shadows had deepened around his eyes. "I won't be able to sleep if I don't clean up."

"The doctor said not to get the cast wet."

"That's why we wrap it in plastic."

"No."

"Yes."

"You're too unsteady. I twisted my ankle last year. I

remember how off balance I felt, how close I came to slipping. No shower until the fever is gone and you can stand without swaying."

He frowned. "I can do that now."

"You think so?" Oh, how the tables turned. "Show me." Jesse hid a smirk from her wounded warrior. In his present mood he definitely wouldn't appreciate her bent for the ironic. Karma did have a way of circling back around.

Not giving an inch, she told him, "Tell you what, if you can walk using only one crutch from here to the bedroom door and back again without losing your balance—" she figured the round trip at about twenty feet "—I'll let you take a shower."

He turned his head, and only his head, to evaluate the distance, and his scowl deepened. His gaze returned to her.

"You're not the boss of me. I can take a shower if I want."

"I'm not the boss of you? What are you, five?" No holding back her smile this time. "You're just surly because you're so weak I could take you. And you know it."

"I'm fine. I just don't have my land legs back yet."

"And you won't have them in the shower, either." She gentled her tone. "Give it up. Why don't you lie down, and I'll give you a bed bath."

His expression went from harassed to ferocious. "I don't want you giving me a bed bath. I want a shower."

Poor Brock. Jesse sighed and relaxed her militant stance. He truly was miserable. And the longer he stood on his bad leg, the more weak and miserable he became. But the man was just stubborn enough to take her on.

"All right, then." She reached for the top button on her teal-and-white striped shirt. "I'm not going to let you get in the shower alone, so if you have to do this, I'll join you."

"What?" He looked like a deer caught in the headlights. Then he blinked, and twin balls of red decorated his cheeks. "You want to get in the shower with me?"

He was blushing. Which was startling enough and an event worth thinking about, but at the moment it just served to remind her how pale he was. And now as she looked closer, she saw beads of moisture on his forehead and under his lower lip.

The Energizer Bunny was definitely running on low.

"I'd prefer it if you'd lie down and let me give you a bed bath, but if getting you to bed is only going to happen by way of a shower, then we need to get moving. Because if you go down, there's no way I can get you back up again."

Her fingers went to the next button on her shirt and his eyes followed. She freed the closure and headed for the third.

Brock just swallowed his tongue. The sight of all that creamy white skin heated his senses and drained the blood from his head. He couldn't think, let alone make sense.

Exactly when had he lost control of the situation? Damn infection had a fever coming and going all day. He stank, his skin itched and now he was sweating. All he wanted was a shower not World War III.

He started to slip when she loosed the next button and the shirt parted to reveal a depth of creamy skin lightly dusted with pale freckles and the hint of cleavage. He desired nothing more than to play connect the dots with his tongue.

Her offer to shower with him short-circuited his synapses. Besides a bed bath being inadequate, he hadn't wanted it because the thought of having her touching him all over, even in an impersonal way, was more than he could handle. Add naked, wet and soapy to the equation; yeah, he saw that picture, completed by him in a cast with a hard-on.

Not happening.

The next button opened right over of her pretty breasts. Her beige lace bra cupped and lifted the soft white flesh offering up the bounty of her plump breasts that flirted with him from behind the lace. The last of the blood drained from his head.

When she reached for the next button, he surrendered.

"Okay, you win." He swung away from the sight of all that lushness. "I'll have a bed bath. But I'll do it myself. Can you bring me some water, soap and towels?"

"Coming right up." At least she didn't gloat. "Go ahead and lie down. I'll be back in a minute."

Brock reached the bed and sat with a sigh. It did feel good to be off his feet. Sighing again, he set the crutches against the wall near the bed.

Being weak sucked.

Losing his career sucked more. He needed to be on his feet getting better, not lounging around feeling sorry for himself and lusting after his wife.

Too soon she came back carrying a plastic basin of water. A couple of towels were tossed over her shoulder and a soap dispenser hung from her jeans pocket. Pretty and efficient. Even as he cursed under his breath he appreciated the package.

She'd only redone one button.

She set the basin on the floor, then stood to place the soap on the bedside table.

"What a beautiful piece." She picked up his old-fashioned pocket watch. "This looks like a true antique. Too bad the glass is broken."

"It is. This watch belonged to my great-great-grandfather. My grandfather gave it to me before he died." Brock treasured the watch as a memento of Grandpa's. He and each of his brothers had been given an old-fashioned timepiece on their tenth birthdays. The watch and the tradition provided a tangible connection to a family he'd denied himself.

"It worked before the accident. That's when the glass broke."

"What a shame." She carefully set it back on the table. "Do you think you'll be able to get it fixed?"

"I hope so." But he'd still carry it even if it couldn't be fixed. It signified too much love for him to give it up.

"Can you stand up for a minute so I can put one of the towels under you?" Jesse got back to the business at hand.

He reached for the crutches but she'd stepped into his way to move the basin out of his path. When she turned back, she saw his dilemma and handed him one of the crutches. He didn't want to appear a wimp by asking for the other crutch, so he put his weight on the one and levered himself up.

And of course she had to touch him. She put one hand under his left elbow and the other on his forearm until he got his balance.

"I got it, thanks," he said.

She made quick work of spreading a towel over the bedspread and then suggested he remove his sweatpants before sitting again. He wore boxers beneath the sweats so he agreed. The sweatpants took some maneuvering, but a final tug landed them around his ankles. Then he needed her help to step out of them.

Finally he lowered himself back to the edge of the bed. Then, ready to get the bath over with, he grabbed the back of his T-shirt and pulled it over his head. When he came out the other side and saw Jesse squeezing soap on a sponge, it took everything he had in him to keep from snapping at her.

Why didn't she understand his need to be alone? He knew she wanted to help, but enough was enough.

"Jesse," he said through gritted teeth. "I can take it from here."

She turned to him, sponge held aloft, and sighed. "At least let me do your back and lower legs. You won't be able to reach either."

He scrubbed a hand over his whiskers, fighting back frustration. It only made it worse that she was right. Mentally he weighed the need to be clean against suffering the temptation of her touch.

Cleanliness won, but only because his pride wouldn't let him admit she affected him to the degree his body was beginning to whisper to him.

"Okay," he conceded. Then watched in awe as she sank gracefully to her knees in front of him and began to wash his feet.

Lord, it felt good, the warm water and soap, the soft rasp of the sponge over his skin, the torment of her touch. She worked steadily, her fingers both strong and utterly gentle, especially when she cleaned the toes of his injured leg.

She reminded him of an ancient handmaiden tending to her lord.

She'd tamed the lush glory of her hair into a ponytail with the long length of it falling over her shoulder in a cascade of red curls. As she leaned forward, her half-undone blouse gaped open affording him a grand view of her bra and all it contained.

"Ugh," he groaned and leaned back on the heels of his hands, looking away from all that temptation.

Now fully aroused, he did nothing to hide the fact. If she insisted on getting up close and personal to assist him, she deserved to know what she'd be working with.

"I'm sorry." Her hands stilled and her brown gaze, potent as whiskey, shot to his face. "Did I hurt you?"

"No. It feels good."

Her cheeks turned bright pink as her gaze shot to his lap. She smiled shyly and went back to the bathroom for fresh water. Her unfailing good humor amazed him. Particularly as he'd been such a Grinch.

He cleared his throat when she came back. "Listen, I know I've been a bear all day."

She placed the basin down and glanced up at him. With a quirk of her lips and one eyebrow, she managed to convey her amused agreement of his self-assessment.

Right. "I really do appreciate all you've done."

"I like being able to do for you." Rising to her feet, she motioned for him sit up so she could reach his back. When he leaned forward she placed a knee next to his hip and half climbed onto the bed.

He frowned, reading a sense of duty into her response. He knew she felt she owed him, which was bull. She'd given him more over the past year and a half than he'd come close to giving her. She'd shared her thoughts, her soul, her daughter with him.

Though two oceans and thousands of miles separated them, she'd given him a home.

His job had been all he'd had for so long, duty and doing it well was all that mattered. He'd forgotten the cause behind it, the connection of why he worked and fought in the Navy. To provide freedom and protection for those he loved but couldn't claim.

Her scent surrounded him, pulling him from his thoughts. The softest trace of vanilla mixed with a whole lot of woman. Mmm, mmm, good.

The sponge stroked down his spine from neck to waist, then reversed and went back up. Then she scrubbed from shoulder to shoulder before moving downward again. It was a sensual massage designed to drive him crazy.

"Brock," she said, a new seriousness in her tone, "why didn't you tell me you could have been killed?"

In a flash his shoulders went from relaxed to rigid. He shook his head. "There was nothing to tell."

"Being crushed doesn't sound like nothing."

Was that recrimination he heard?

"Is this about Emily's little scene?" Brock didn't want to talk about this. He hadn't explained himself in eighteen years. He saw no reason to start now. Time he reminded her theirs was a noncommitted relationship. "Forget that. It doesn't apply to us."

The sponge stopped moving as she went very still behind him. "The truth isn't exclusive to marriage. I care about what happens to you."

He looked over his shoulder at her. "You know everything you need to know."

Hurt, deep and wrenching, entered her eyes. She looked down to hide her reaction from him. She concentrated on her hands as if trying to remember what she'd been doing. Retreating from the bed, she dropped the sponge in the basin of water.

"Call me when you're done." He heard the near break in her voice. To offset it, she angled her chin, set her shoulders and, proud as a queen, headed for the door. "I'll come back to clean up."

She paused with her hand on the doorknob and looked back at him with a blank expression. "I know we don't have what Emily and Jake have between them, but I thought we were friends. I thought it was okay to care whether you lived or died. I'm sorry to learn I was wrong."

CHAPTER NINE

JESSE lightly hummed a lullaby as she lowered a sleeping Allie into her crib. The baby slept through the night most nights, but Brock's arrival a week ago had disrupted her schedule.

Allie spent the mornings with Jesse's neighbor's teenage daughter. A junior in high school, Erika welcomed the chance to make money over the holidays. She liked working the mornings because she said her friends weren't up and ready to do anything before noon, anyway.

Jesse had taken leave from the preschool as soon as she heard about Brock's accident, to be available to care for him, but she'd actually already had Erika lined up for babysitting duty before Brock's accident. Jesse had planned to use the time to study and complete her two Internet classes on early-childhood development.

Instead, she used the mornings to take Brock to his outpatient appointments and did her studying at night.

She'd just turned out the light tonight when Allie first stirred.

Hopefully, Brock would get the all-clear tomorrow, or rather later this morning. She couldn't believe the progress he'd made in a week. The fever and infection were gone. Thank goodness. Which meant his strength grew daily. And he managed his crutches well enough to get in her way daily.

Allie fussed a bit, missing the warmth and soothing motion of her mother's arms. Jesse continued to hum and pat the baby gently, before slowly easing away.

As she stood watching Allie to make sure she stayed asleep, Jesse couldn't remember the last time she'd slept until noon. Probably not since the first night she spent in the condo when Brock brought her here from the hospital.

It seemed a lifetime ago.

Leaving the door open a crack, Jesse moved to the living room and her makeshift bed on the couch. When she'd made the second bedroom into a nursery, she'd elected to put the bed in storage and keep Brock's weights and workout gear set up.

It didn't make sense, but it had seemed such an intrusion to remove his personal gym.

She climbed under the sheet—she'd already tossed the blanket aside—and curled on her side, glad she'd made the decision she had. Yesterday Brock talked about using the equipment to keep in shape while convalescing.

She'd learned one thing over the past week. Lord, she was in trouble. He drove her nuts, irascible one moment, distant the next, and always, always a sexy beast.

She worried for the state of her heart when even at his worst she longed for his company.

After his emotional rebuff that first night, she'd kept her responses to him cool. Still it had been an effort. He'd hurt her, but she missed him. Every day for nearly a year and a half she'd shared her thoughts with him. It was hard to just turn that off.

Harder still to ignore his brooding intensity, his steely muscles, his raw masculinity. She wanted to touch him, to taste him, to linger with him. She wanted everything she couldn't have.

And he absolutely adored Allie. No matter how uncomfortable or irritated he was, he always handled the baby with gentleness and care. For that alone, Jesse would forgive him much.

A sound down the hall caught her attention. She sat up to listen for Allie and instead met Brock's gaze through the darkness.

Using his crutches, he limped forward to perch a hip on the back of the couch and reach out a hand to trail a finger along a loose curl. "Why are you sleeping on the couch?"

Jesse moved away from his touch. She might be a sucker for his company but that didn't mean she'd make it easy on him.

"Why are you up?" She scooted back then leaned

against the arm of the couch, allowing her some distance from his heat, from his clean, male scent.

"Water. Your turn to answer my question."

She sighed. "I put the spare bed in storage when I set up the crib."

"Why'd you do that? I told you to put the weight equipment away." He scrubbed his knuckles over his whiskers. "I guess this explains why you didn't remind me we needed to get the gear from storage."

"Exactly. I know how going to the gym on the ship helped relax you. I wanted you to have equipment available when you got home. And it's not as if anyone ever used the bed."

The statement hung in the air between them. The question of their unresolved relationship a trumpeting elephant in the room.

Moonlight filtered in through gauzy drapes, slanting across the bare expanse of Brock's chest, defining muscles with light and shadow. She longed to reach out and touch, with her fingers, her lips, her tongue. She wanted to trace the hard line of his pecs, taste the salt of his skin, tease the hard nubs of his nipples.

Were they as sensitive as hers? She tucked the sheet closer under her arms, aware her nipples had puckered in response to her thoughts.

Why did she continue to put herself through this torture? Maybe the time had come for them to have the dreaded conversation.

"Brock—"

"Jesse—"

They spoke at the same moment. Jesse's heartbeat jumped. Call her a coward, but she latched on to the opportunity to delay the inevitable.

"You go," she said.

"This is ridiculous." He waved a hand indicating the tangle of blankets at the end of the couch. "No wonder you've had shadows under your eyes. You're not going to get a decent night's sleep on this rack."

"You're exaggerating. The shadows are there because I've been studying before going to sleep and Allie's had a couple of restless nights." She thumped the sheet-covered cushion. "This couch is plenty comfortable."

"It's too short and it's leather, which means on a warm night like this it's probably like sleeping in a swamp."

Yeah, that about described it. "It's not that bad. And it's not like I have a lot of choice."

"You could sleep in the bed with me."

Her heart stopped, then quick-started into overdrive. "I'm pretty sure that wouldn't be a good idea."

"We're both adults. And I'm practically immobile in this cast."

"Yeah, but I'm not." Damn. Damn. Damn. Did she just say that out loud?

The amused and slightly surprised look on Brock's face told her, "Yes." The passion that quickly tightened his features told her, "Oh, yeah!"

How stupid could she get? Talk about mixed signals. She turned him down one moment and propositioned him the next.

So much for playing the uninterested card, or for dealing with the end of their relationship.

Well, this could be a good thing. Either she'd finally get a good night's sleep, and maybe a little more, or…or Brock was not interested at all, and at least she would know for sure.

"I'm sure you can control yourself," he said, sending her hopes skidding. "And if not, I guess I'm willing to take that risk."

Reining in her emotions, she crossed her arms over her chest and contemplated him. All that passionate intensity aimed her way and that nonanswer was the best he could come up with?

"And if it's not a risk I'm willing to take?" She challenged him.

He leaned forward and tugged on her loose curl. "Coward."

With that challenge, he propped the crutches under his arms and got up to go for his water. He just walked away. His utter gall made her blood boil.

It was one thing to call *herself* a coward, but she wouldn't let *him* get away with it.

Jesse tossed the sheet aside and stormed after him, uncaring she wore only boy-cut briefs and a spaghetti-strap camisole. She advanced on him as he opened the refrigerator and removed a bottle of water. Her hand on the front panel added extra force to the closing of the refrigerator door.

"What was that?" She swung her arm toward the living room.

Leaning on one crutch, he worked the cap loose. "That was a commonsense suggestion for an unexpected problem."

He sipped his water, appearing way too cool and collected, considering their conversation. Well, if you didn't count the tent in his shorts. Which only confused her further, causing her ire to grow more.

"I'm not just talking about the suggestion. I'm talking about your ping-pong signals. Touching me, inviting me to your bed, calling me a coward when I hesitate. But when I practically proposition you, you turn away. And the whole time, you're so hard you can hardly reach the refrigerator handle."

He laughed, a rough, joyful sound. "Now that's an exaggeration."

"I'm serious, Brock. I want you, but I need to know where we stand."

"And I want you, too, Jesse." He cupped her cheek, caressed her with his thumb. "I always have, and this time around there's nothing to distract me from imagining you naked."

His gaze swept over her in a heated wave of lust so blatant not even the darkness disguised it, reminding her of the little she wore. Naked, no; the next thing to it, yeah.

"But I control my urges. They don't control me. And we have one huge complication we can't ignore."

She sighed. Of course they did. "We're married."

"Yeah. You'd think it would simplify the matter but it only makes it harder. I don't want to take advantage of you, Jesse."

"You wouldn't be." Why was she pursuing him so fiercely? Hadn't she been worrying about the safety of her heart not twenty minutes ago?

Uh-huh. But that was twenty minutes before he said he wanted her, too.

This may be her only opportunity to be with him. And everything in her, physically and emotionally, craved him. Everything in him called to her—his intelligence, his dry humor, his dedication and loyalty. She longed to step into his strong arms and lose herself to the passion she tried so diligently to deny.

Did she want their marriage to be real? Did she love him? Honestly, she didn't know, but she welcomed a chance to find out.

"Jesse." He set her away from him. "You need to know I'm not the commitment type. People who rely on me are always disappointed."

She stared at him, unable to believe her ears.

"What hogwash. Bar none, you are the most reliable, steadfast person I've ever known." Insulted, she turned and walked back to the couch.

"You don't need to make things up to discourage me," she informed him, proud that the words came out steady around the tears lodged in her throat. "I'm a big girl, I can take rejection."

"This isn't about rejection." He limped after her, watching with brooding eyes as she reclaimed her spot on the couch. "It's about expectations." His voice had grown hoarse. Gruff with emotion? "You were right the other night. I do think of you as a friend. The Lord knows you made the long, lonely absence bearable." He cleared his throat. "I care about you. Care about our friendship. I couldn't stand to see you hurt."

She looked him straight in the eyes. "Being with you has never hurt me." She lay down, pulled the sheet up to her shoulder and turned her back to him. "It's when you push me away that it hurts."

Brock swung along on his crutches, trailing Jesse and Allie through the large commissary. He'd tagged along on the shopping trip rather than spend one more boring day in the recliner.

He'd never been one for TV, so other than working with the weights and surfing the Internet there was little to do around the house. He worked the weights twice a day, focusing on his upper body. Unfortunately none of it occupied his thoughts to the extent he could put Jesse and her artic shoulder out of his mind.

Packed as they were in such close quarters, they practically tripped over each other every few minutes. And when they did, she evaded his gaze, dodged away from any physical contact and politely, oh, so politely, excused herself.

His teeth ground together. As if he and she were nothing more than strangers. It made him want to chew gravel.

Didn't she realize he was trying to protect her?

"Hey, Sullivan," a voice hailed him from half a row away.

Brock looked from the sway of Jesse's hips to the row on his right but didn't stop walking. He'd almost caught up to her. Spying an old colleague, he waved but kept moving forward.

Up ahead Jesse had paused and turned to look his way. Probably heard his name called. Her name, too, he guessed. Funny it should strike him now that she'd been using his name for a year and a half, yet the novelty of it was so new to him.

What did it mean that instead of discomfort, he took satisfaction in her using his name?

"Brock," she said as he drew closer. "You don't have to roll around with me. You can stay and talk to your friends. I don't mind. But if I don't keep moving, we'll be here all day."

Stunning in pink and black, she drew him like steel to a magnet. He'd much rather keep her company than rehash his recent history yet again.

"I'm tired of explaining myself to my friends."

"They care about you, Brock. They're just showing concern."

"Yeah, well I've already stopped three times, explained my injury three times, tried to be positive about an uncertain future three times. Enough, already."

Her expression froze, all compassion draining away. "I guess these are just a few more people you'll be disappointing."

He stilled, stung by her attack.

"Jesse—"

"No." She stopped with a hand on his chest, remorse replacing the freeze. "That was petty and uncalled for. I'm sorry."

"Me, too." He looked away from her, unwilling to reveal how weary he suddenly felt. "Maybe this trip was premature."

"Okay." She glanced at the few items in the cart, automatically removing her keys from Allie's grip. "I just need to get a few more things for the baby, then we can go. Why don't you go get a soda at the food court? I'll meet you there when I'm done."

Allie protested the loss of the keys with a loud wail. Jesse tried to distract her with a teething ring in the shape of a rabbit, but Allie wanted the keys.

"Come here, baby." Brock lifted the little girl into his arms, taking delight in her slight weight against his chest. Her unconditional trust and affection smoothed the sharp edges of his temper. "You want to come with Daddy? I'll get you some ice cream."

"Brock." Jesse's tone held a note of caution.

"A fruit bar," he reassured her. "It'll feel good on her gums."

"You amaze me." Jesse ran her finger over Allie's cheek. The baby was all smiles now she'd gained release from the cart. "How are you going to carry her with your crutches?"

"I'm not." He handed her one of his crutches then crossed the aisle to snag a deserted cart. He placed the baby in, put the crutch back in the main section, then used the cart as support to return to her for the other crutch, which also went into the cart. "All set."

"Pretty clever." Jesse smiled her approval. "Try not to spoil her."

"Uh, no." Utterly unrepentant, he refused to follow her advice. "Can't make that promise. But take your time. Allie will run interference for me until you get done."

Jesse watched Brock roll away with Allie after warning her of the evils of shopping and that no matter what anyone said no one needed more than one pair of black heels.

Jesse grinned at that. No doubt he'd found her rather extensive collection of black shoes in the closet.

The smile slowly faded as she pushed the cart down the detergent aisle. Brock showed such patience and tenderness toward the baby and, until his return, toward Jesse. And despite the new tension between them, he'd never once made her feel as if she were a duty he felt put upon to undertake.

She knew how demeaning it felt to be an obligation, the smallness of it, the tear to the soul that only lack of self-worth could inflict.

She'd vowed never to be anyone's duty ever again.

Only for her child's welfare had she wavered from that promise.

When she accepted Brock's proposal, she'd known his offer came from a misplaced sense of duty. She'd been prepared to live with the indignity in exchange for his help, for the home and medical benefits necessary to save her child.

Before their hormones had interfered, he'd only ever been tolerant and giving. Okay, yeah, when he had a plan or wanted something to happen he had the manners of a dictator, but down deep he had a good heart.

The man would give his right arm before letting anyone down. For him to claim he failed those who relied on him boggled her mind. Did he truly believe that? Or had he manufactured the vice to create distance between them?

She wished she knew.

Thirty minutes later she reached the checkout. Brock appeared in time to help unload the cart. The clerk announced the total, and Jesse asked Brock to hand her her purse.

"I got it." He fished out his wallet, flipped it open and pulled out some cash. Along with the money, a photo came out and floated, faceup, onto the counter.

Jesse's eyes about popped out of her head.

In full color, the photo showcased her kneeling on the end of a bed wearing a black teddi made of lace and strings. Red hair mussed, lips painted a tempting rose, skin creamy white against the black lingerie, the stark contrasts instantly drew the eye.

"Oh my God." Appalled, she made a grab for the photo.

"That's mine." Brock beat her to it, swiping up the picture and placing it back in his wallet.

The heat of embarrassment flooded Jesse's cheeks. Avoiding the cashier's gaze, she rushed Brock through the rest of the transaction, and as soon as they were out of hearing, demanded, "How did you get that picture?"

He sent her an odd sidelong glance out of the corner of his eye. "You sent it to me."

"I didn't." The denial came fast and sure.

She knew of the photo, of course. A few of the chiefs' wives got together last February and decided to send their men boudoir shots for Valentine's Day. Wanting to keep up appearances, Jesse had gone along with the plan, but she'd never sent the pictures.

"How did I get it if you didn't send it to me?"

"Emily," Jesse muttered. She explained about the wives' Valentine's Day surprise. "Emily knew I didn't send the pictures."

When Emily had asked about Brock's reaction, wanting to share in the excitement of surprising the men, Jesse confessed she hadn't sent them. She used the excuse of not having lost all her baby fat. Which was true, except she actually thought the weight looked good on her.

"I only went along with the plan because the wives

still think of us as newlyweds. But I never intended sending the pictures. I told Emily I thought the photos made me look pale and top heavy. She replied they made me look lush and sexy as hell. She must have sent the pictures because she thought I was too bashful to send them myself."

And Brock had never said a word to Jesse about receiving them.

Jesse fumed as she transferred Allie from the cart to her car seat. At the back of the SUV, Brock awkwardly loaded the groceries. When she was done with Allie, Jesse walked to the back.

"You all right?" Brock asked as she joined him.

"Just dandy. For someone who just flashed a grandmother at the checkout. Give me the photo." She held out her hand palm up.

If she got the picture back maybe she could pretend this moment never happened.

He looked from her hand to her face. "No."

"Brock."

"No." He dropped the keys in her open palm. "Emily's right, you look sexy as hell." Turning, he swung himself around the vehicle to climb in the passenger side.

Gritting her teeth, she took her seat behind the wheel. She'd tried so hard these past few days to keep her cool around him. But she couldn't be cool about this.

She felt raw and exposed.

A tornado of emotions stormed within her, anger,

betrayal, embarrassment, pain, confusion. Of course Emily meant well, but the interference put Jesse in an untenable position.

"Oh my God." Suddenly weary, Jesse let her head fall forward to rest on the padded steering wheel. "No wonder you invented commitment issues to avoid me. You probably think I'm stalking you."

"I don't think it's possible to stalk someone from three thousand miles away."

"Please don't joke. I'm mortified here."

"Why?" The heat of his hand came to rest on the nape of her neck, strong fingers working at the knot of tension. "You're beautiful in the pictures, a sensual goddess better than any pinup poster."

"You're just making it worse." If possible her cheeks heated even more. When she thought of the come-hither poses caught on film, she cringed inside. She turned her head to the side, sent him a glance of entreaty. "Please give back the pictures."

His hand stilled on her neck.

"Why?" His expression took on the quality of granite. "Were they meant for someone else?" He held her gaze in an intense connection. "Who were you thinking about when the camera took the picture, Jesse?"

CHAPTER TEN

"You," Jesse told Brock. "I was thinking of you. Of the kiss you gave me on the dock before you left."

His eyes lit with a brilliant blue fire. She saw his intent before he made his first move.

"I've thought of that kiss, too. And of you. Wondering if I'd ever get a chance to taste you again." He tightened his hand on the back of her neck and drew her to him.

Jesse met him halfway, sealing her mouth to his.

It was like one of those movie moments where the couple on screen flew together as if unable to stand being apart an instant longer. And where the audience sighed with satisfaction.

Jesse would sigh but she was too busy.

Tongues met in a desperate dance of acquaintance. He angled his head, taking the kiss deeper, stealing her breath, heating her passion.

He tasted better than she remembered, felt better. She dug her fingers into his short, crisp hair and held him to her, nipping his lower lip in sensual play. He answered by pulling her further over the gearshift and plundering her mouth like a pirate going after treasure.

Finally the discomfort of the gear shift poking her in the hip, and yes, the need to breathe, caused her to pull back.

Brock barely let her up for air before pulling her back for another hard kiss. When he released her, they both fell back in their seats.

Too buzzed to drive, she turned over the ignition and set the air conditioner on full blast.

"I need to talk to you, so you understand some stuff." Brock reached for her hand, brought her fingers to his mouth. "Let's go get some lunch, and I'll tell you about Sherry."

She looked from where his mouth nibbled her fingers to his eyes. "Who's Sherry?"

"My fiancée."

"We met in high school," Brock said after the waitress left them.

Jesse nodded, her concentration on him as she reached into Allie's bag and took out a small container of baby food.

Needing something to occupy his hands and his attention, he took the plastic dish of fruit from her and picked up a spoon.

"Sherry was a cheerleader and I was into sports. We hooked up as freshmen. Graduated together, went on to college. We had our lives together all planned out."

"Childhood sweethearts," Jesse said softly.

"You could say that." He fed a bite of peaches to Allie. "She stole my heart with her first smile. From that moment on there was no one else for me. Or for her. We were perfect together."

"No arguments? No high school jealousies?" she asked. "Life is full of drama at that age."

"No." He shook his head as he swiped Allie's mouth with a napkin, briefly looking up to meet Jesse's curious gaze. "That's what made it so great to be with her. My whole life was drama. I'd lost my parents the year before, went to live with my grandmother."

He and his five brothers, but he couldn't tell Jesse that. He'd never mentioned his family to her. At first she'd been too much a stranger. And once he knew her better, knew how estranged she felt in her own home and how much she longed for a loving family of her own, he couldn't tell her he'd blown his place in the best family in the world.

And he couldn't go there now.

It took all his control to talk about Sherry. But Jesse deserved to know his resistance came from his own failings and not anything she did or said.

"Sherry was a haven for me. She brought me peace." He shot Jesse a wicked grin. "And got me hot all at the same time."

She bowed her head to him. "Quite a talented woman."

"Yeah." Another bite for Allie. "She had long blond

hair and the biggest green eyes. And she had me wrapped around her little finger."

"Brock." Jesse's hand settled over his, warm and comforting. "What happened?"

"An accident. Our second year of college. We came home for Thanksgiving. We were supposed to stay overnight, but Sherry had to work the next day and she decided she wanted to go home so she could get something done in the morning."

He took a bite of the peaches, making Allie laugh. God, he loved her innocence, her sweet nature. He never wanted anything bad to touch her.

Or her mother.

Jesse squeezed his hand, encouraging him to continue.

"I wanted to stay. It was foggy and I hadn't seen my grandmother for a while." Or his brothers. He'd missed the camaraderie, the one-upmanship, the fun of being with them.

"But she insisted, and as usual I gave in."

"Did you argue? Is that what caused the accident?"

"No, but it was late by then. I was tired. The fog was thick."

"Oh, Brock."

"I rounded a turn, and there in the middle of the road was a deer. I swerved right, but Sherry grabbed the wheel and jerked." He'd never told anyone that before, about Sherry grabbing the wheel, not to the police and not to their families. "We raced off the road and into a tree. Sherry died instantly."

From one spinning moment to the next he lost everything, his fiancée, his future and his family's respect.

"I'm so sorry." Jesse breathed her sorrow. "How tragic."

"Yeah, tragic." Despair thickened his voice. "She was so beautiful, so full of life, and I killed her."

"Brock, no. You said it yourself, it was an accident."

"I agreed to leave when the conditions were bad. I was the driver. I was responsible." His older brother Alex hammered that notion home. Barely conscious in the hospital, Brock had listened to his brother rant and rave, his anger tangible in the sterile room. The words hurt more than the broken arm and bruises Brock suffered from the accident.

"And Sherry changed the plans, plus she grabbed the wheel, yet you don't blame her. No one was responsible. It was an accident."

"It could have been avoided."

"You know better." Compassion and understanding couldn't hide the bite in her voice. "What-ifs and could-have-beens have no place in this world. They're a waste of time, energy and emotion."

"And sometimes they house a bitter truth that avoidance only perpetuates."

"No," she disagreed, sitting back as the waitress placed a plate in front of her. "They keep you in the past while the future waits with such promise."

"Not for me." Brock stared at his plate of steak sandwich and fries with a total lack of appetite.

"You made one wrong decision in your youth, so you're to be punished for the rest of your life?"

"It seems only fair. Sherry lost the rest of her life because of that decision."

"And is that the advice you'd give one of your sailors?" she asked with cutting precision. "Make one mistake and give up? I don't think so."

"We're not talking about one of my sailors."

"We may as well be, you're making as much sense as a raw recruit. Brock, you're a rational, intelligent, giving man. Honor and duty define you. Yes, you lost a love, but beyond that I think this hurt has stayed with you because it goes against your very nature."

Brock stared at her. Her words resonated on a visceral level. Was it possible she saw him more clearly than his own brother?

No, that was just wishful thinking on his part.

But he couldn't deny it felt good to have someone arguing his side for a change.

Sweat rolled down Brock's neck as he systematically worked on his triceps, then his quads. He went through the regime three times a day. The upper-body strength helped him with the crutches, increasing his maneuverability and his balance. He also worked his good leg and completed the exercises suggested by his physician.

The workout sessions gave him the illusion of control, of having a say in his recuperation, his future.

He wasn't good at being helpless, and this kept him sane.

Plus it was something to do.

And it afforded him a great view of Jesse at work.

From the workout bench in Allie's room, he had a partial view of the kitchen and living room. A peek into her world.

The woman never stopped. She did all the cooking, kept the house clean and tidy, studied incessantly and saw to all Allie's needs. His, too, come to that.

Well almost all.

Her laughter floated to him from the kitchen where she sat feeding Allie her dinner. The sound of her joy caused a shiver of awareness to run down his spine. Watching her with the baby always filled him with a sense of satisfaction. Together they were so beautiful, so serene. A unit. Yet he never felt left out.

If he were to walk out there right now, they would gather him into their inner circle, invite him to share in their delight.

He lowered the dumbbells to the floor and reached for a towel to wipe his face. In the kitchen Allie puckered up and Jesse leaned down for a sticky kiss. She came away with a handprint on her cheek and licking her lips. Allie giggled when Jesse pretended to eat her up.

Brock smiled at their antics. And in that moment it struck him, he'd done something really right here. In helping Jesse, in providing a safe nest for Allie, he'd put something astonishing in motion.

Jesse just astounded him. Her drive and intelligence, her dedication and honesty blew him away. She made him think, made him laugh, made him sweat.

He no longer thought of her as too young. When he looked at her, he saw a woman. A giving, open, stunning woman. With great listening skills.

Picking up the dumbbells, he placed them back on the rack.

He never spoke about Sherry, preferred to leave the past in the past, but talking with Jesse today had eased something in him. Made him look at the past from a different perspective, a more mature perspective. He didn't know if anything had really changed, but her arguments on his behalf gave him a lot to think about.

Not least of which was the temptation to give in to the heat sparking between them. Oh, yeah, she made him sweat.

But all thoughts of the past and future slid right out of his head when he looked up to see Jesse headed his way with Allie in her arms. Sometime, while he'd been lost in the past, Jesse had obviously made an effort to clean the two of them up because her T-shirt was wet. The pale-pink material clung faithfully to the plump glory of her breasts, the dampness causing her nipples to pucker against the thin cloth.

She appeared in the doorway and grinned at him. "This girl just loves peaches. I don't know who needs a bath more, her or me."

"Peaches are hard to resist." Brock wrapped the towel

around his neck and pushed to his feet. When he reached the doorway, he bent his head and opened his mouth over hers. He sank into her, taking the kiss deep, loving how she rose onto her toes to get closer to him. Finally he pulled back, licked his lips, before sauntering cheekily away; well, as much as the crutches allowed. "Sweet."

Jesse opened Brock's bottom dresser drawer and put in his clean blue jeans. Next came his socks. And then his boxers. With the last came a vision of him in the flimsy garment in all his male glory.

Simple truth, the man drove her nuts. The occasional kisses and constant touches were driving her out of her skin with need.

The memory of how blatantly he'd displayed himself when she gave him the hand bath his first night home flashed into her mind. She'd wanted to lick him up one side and down the other. Not even his pain-induced grouchiness put her off.

At least, not until he deliberately shut her out.

To be dismissed when she felt they'd grown so close hurt more than she'd ever have guessed.

Hearing about Sherry and the loss he suffered explained so much. But she truly thought he'd punished himself long enough. He deserved some happiness.

From the left side of the dresser, she pulled out her preferred night attire, a tank top and lightweight shorts. She'd already put Allie down and now she'd finished the laundry, Jesse could get comfortable and do some studying. One good thing to be said about the rack of a couch, it helped her stay awake.

When she straightened, a glint of gold on the dresser top caught her eye. She reached for it and found she held Brock's pocket watch, the one given to him by his grandfather and damaged in the accident.

The watch had the fine sheen of real gold and the weight of a quality piece. She ran her thumb over the etched back worn smooth by years of use. Intricate scrollwork bordered the edge, and in the center were engraved lavish initials, *ESJ* with the *S* larger and more prominent than the other two letters.

She well knew there was nothing she could ever do to repay Brock for his kindness and sacrifice in marrying her to give her his benefits. But maybe here was something that would have meaning for him. She could get his watch fixed, give him back a part of his history.

"Jesse," Brock said from the doorway.

"Yeah." She turned and almost tripped over the clothes basket at the sight of Brock in a towel, his cast and nothing else. She caught and steadied herself on the edge of the dresser.

Wow. The man possessed a truly magnificent body.

He'd worked with his weights earlier, but he'd been watching a basketball game when she went through the living room.

"I overdid my workout." He ran a hand over the hair on his chest. "I need your help with my shower."

Heat flowed through Jesse as if she already stood under a hot spray of water. Did he mean he needed help as in assistance? Or help as in slick, wet, soapy bodies sharing the same space getting personal and up close?

It was hard to tell what this meant. He rarely admitted to a weakness.

Usually so blunt, she bit back the question. A woman could only take so much rejection. And he hadn't exactly corrected her when she'd mentioned stalking him.

Then again he stood steady and tall in the doorway filling the frame with mere inches to spare. He didn't look as if he needed help with anything.

"Are you feeling light-headed?" she asked, approaching him, feeling her attraction growing with each step closer.

"No." His gaze seared her from head to toe.

"Brock." Helpless, she sighed. If he truly needed assistance, of course she'd help. But if this was a romantic overture, the shower seemed a dangerous choice.

She stopped in front of him. "I'll get my bathing suit."

He slowly shook his head, his gaze never leaving hers. "You don't need your suit."

Oh, heck. She was no good at dodging the issue. She couldn't stand not knowing what he intended.

"Brock, if this is an attempt to get me naked, I'm willing, but with your leg in that cast we'd be better off in the bed than the shower."

"Woman, you see right through me." He circled the

nape of her neck with one warm hand and drew her to him. "Come here."

His mouth claimed hers in a heated melding of lips. No rush this time. He drew the kiss out, softly suckling her tongue, lingering over her sigh, then taking her deeper into sensation with light nibbles and tender strokes.

She ringed her arms around his neck and went up on tiptoe to better match her curves to his hard planes. He leaned back against the door frame and took her weight in full body contact.

When he trailed kisses from the corner of her mouth down the side of her neck to nuzzle the sensitive crook where neck met shoulder, she lost the strength in her knees and slid full into his embrace. He held her with easy strength, his hand trailing up from her waist to cup one breast. She shuddered at his touch.

"Forever." She breathed the word around small bites to his chest. He tasted so good.

"Forever what?" he murmured, delightfully distracted as he paid homage to her left earlobe and the erogenous zone right behind and below her ear.

"That's how long I've waited for this moment—forever."

Stepping to the side, she slid under his right arm and together they made their way to the bed.

Some time later Jesse shivered as Brock trailed a hand down her back and over her hip. Her body still hummed from his sweet loving.

The man possessed some serious moves, moves meant to drive a woman over the edge of reason straight into the wellspring of ecstasy. His care and tenderness, his demands and strength, his command of his body and hers showed her how it was to be with a man instead of a boy.

She sighed, content to be in the arms of her lover. The soft rush of her breath flowed over their entwined bodies.

"You okay?" Brock asked.

"I'm positively fabulous." She fanned her hand over his chest loving the feel of him, warm and firm and hair roughened. "How are you?"

"I can honestly say I haven't felt this good in a year and a half."

Jesse instantly went up on her elbow to look down at him. He did have the look of a satisfied man: mussed hair, relaxed lines, a smile kicking up the corner of his mouth. She liked seeing the furrows of pain gone from his brow.

"A year and a half? Are you saying you haven't been with a woman in all that time? Brock, I never expected that kind of fidelity from you."

He groaned, covering his eyes with one hand. "*Now* you tell me."

"Don't joke," she told him, awed by his revelation. "You've been celibate all this time? I love that, and that's just mean. I got all the benefits from this marriage and now I find you've sacrificed even more. It's not fair."

"Hey." He threaded his fingers through her hair, cupping her head. "It was my choice. Not something you should blame yourself for."

"I don't understand," she whispered. "Why?"

"I discovered I'm traditional when it comes to marriage. How about you?"

"Me, too."

He tightened his hand and his gaze grew focused. "So you haven't been with anyone, either?"

"You're asking me if I was faithful to you?"

"Not to me. To the vows. Our bargain didn't prevent you from seeing someone else."

Amazed by his unexpected dedication, Jesse wondered what he wanted to hear from her. Even three thousand miles away he'd been a huge presence in her life. She had never considered seeing anyone else.

"I promised to protect your reputation," she reminded him.

"Which required discretion not abstinence." He tucked a curl behind her ear, his touch gentle in contrast to the intense curiosity in his blue gaze. "You're awfully twitchy about the question. You can tell me the truth. I'm not going to get mad."

"I'm just wondering how you can even ask the question. I was pregnant for the first seven months, had a baby attached to me for the next six months and I'm still struggling with baby fat. Hardly the most attractive catch out there. And if I was looking for someone, which I haven't been, I spend my days with toddlers and Navy wives. Not many prospects there."

"You work on a Navy base where the ratio of men

to women is about twenty to one. And you're a student at State. You're a young, healthy, beautiful woman. I'm sure you've had opportunities."

"Oh, right." She lifted her chin. "There was this real cute guy in my Lamaze class."

He laughed and then drew her to him for a fast, hard kiss. "Brat."

"You bet." She took advantage of the new position to initiate a kiss of her own, a slower more in-depth kiss. When she pulled back she stayed close, ran a finger over his slick lower lip. "I think you would get mad if I confessed to a liaison with another man. I think you're jealous."

"Is it that obvious?" He rolled his head on the pillow and looked up at the ceiling.

"It's flattering." She bit his chin. "But unnecessary. The truth is there hasn't been another man for me since I fell at your feet in the Green Garter."

"Jesse, your honesty floors me." He pulled her on top of him, cradling her head on his chest. "I wish I was the man you think I am, instead of a broken man with a fractured past and an uncertain future."

"And I wish you could see yourself as clearly as I see you. Maybe then you'd have faith in yourself to find the right path whether you stay in the Navy or not."

He was silent for a while, his fingers slowly stirring through her hair, fanning the red strands over his chest. When he finally spoke, what he shared nearly broke her heart.

"I'm a sailor. The Navy has been my home for seventeen years. If I lose that, I'm not sure I'll know who I am."

CHAPTER ELEVEN

BROCK found the birthday card in the bedroom waste-basket.

"What's this?" he said aloud to Allie.

Without hesitation he plucked the card out of the trash and read it. Besides the Hallmark sentiment it simply said "Jessica, happy birthday" and was signed "Your Parents."

Damn her parents. No words of love; not even a show of family in the form of "Mom and Dad," just "Your Parents." How could such cold people have created such a generous, loving, honest woman?

Allie reached for the card, but Brock tossed it back in the trash.

"Your grandparents are contemptible fools."

Jesse deserved so much better. And no one better to give it to her than him. And her birthday provided the perfect opportunity.

"When is your mama's birthday? Yesterday, today, tomorrow?" How was it possible he didn't know? At least he knew her age, twenty-five. He thought back to the young, frightened girl he had left behind. She'd blossomed into a beautiful, competent woman capable of handling a child and a home all on her own.

"Emily will know. We'll call her. I'm sure she'd be willing to watch you, too, so I can give Mama a special night to remember."

He tucked the crutch under his left arm, hefted Allie higher against his chest and headed toward her room.

"It'll be our secret. Maybe Emily will keep you all night, would you like that? Then Mama can sleep late in the morning. Daddy would like that."

Allie clapped her hands, reacting more to his tone than the words, but he took it as agreement.

"Right. It's a plan."

Brock was up to something. Jesse recognized his take-charge mode. An energy vibed off him whenever he was in the thick of it or waiting for his plans to gel.

She looked up from where she was studying on the couch, first checking Allie where she played quietly in the playpen, then turning to watch Brock. He sat at the dining room table reading his mail, yet the room practically hummed with static.

Oh, yeah. He was up to something.

A knock sounded at the door. For some reason a thrill of anticipation ran through her. Something, maybe the way he looked at his watch, told her his plotting had to do with whoever was at the door.

"Are you expecting anyone?" she asked as she rose to her feet.

"No, but Allie is."

Jesse stopped and faced him. "What?"

He gestured with his chin. "Answer the door."

Confused but intrigued, she did as he suggested and found Emily and her two youngest sons on the doorstep.

"Hey, Jesse." The boys, five and seven, chorused as they sauntered by. Then they spotted Brock at the table. "Uncle Brock!"

The boys ran to the dining room to admire Brock's cast.

"Hey, girl." Emily, looking radiant in maternity jeans and a red sleeveless shirt, followed behind the boys at a slow waddle. "You better get dressed. Your car is waiting at the curb."

"My car?" Jesse hugged her friend in greeting. "It's in the carport."

"Not that car silly. The limo."

"Limo?" Jesse felt like Alice sliding down the rabbit hole. "What limo?" She stuck her head outside the door and, sure enough, a white stretch limousine sat on the street out front.

"Oops." Emily looked sheepish. "Did I spoil the surprise? Busted. Happy birthday." Emily threw her arms around Jesse in a huge hug and promptly burst into tears.

"Hey, it's all right." Jesse hugged her friend, patting her back. Jesse looked to Brock for help.

"No," Emily wailed. "Your man's taking you out all

fancy and special. And I must be late because the car is already here."

"Uh-oh. There go Mom's waterworks again." Seven-year-old Troy returned to his mother's side. He stood patting her back, a comforting gesture he'd obviously done before.

"Yep," his younger brother confirmed. "It's the sprinklers."

"Hush, you two," Jesse admonished them. "Can't you see your mother is upset?"

"She's fine," Brock assured everyone as he took Emily into his arms. "Everything is just fine."

Jesse admired his gumption; not many men braved a woman's tears let alone a pregnant woman's tears.

Emily wrapped herself around Brock. "I spoiled your surprise."

"Not at all. You're the best part of the surprise. Boys, can you run and get Allie's bag. It's in her room by the dresser."

"Sure." The brothers raced away.

Jesse heard a whimper and turned to get Allie from the playpen before she started to cry, too. "It's okay, sweet pea. Emily's just crying baby tears."

"That's exactly right." Brock led Emily to the couch, handed her a couple of tissues. "No need to be upset. You're right on time. The car is early. But now you can stay and help Jesse get ready."

"I'd like that." Emily wiped her eyes, blew her nose. "But what about Allie?"

"The boys can keep her occupied. I'll use her room to get dressed and keep an eye on them. Right boys?"

Troy ran up with Allie's bag over his shoulder, Eric hot on his heels.

"Right," they echoed. "Can we play with her blocks?"

"See." Brock bent to kiss Emily's cheek. "Everyone's happy."

"O-okay." Emily smiled. "I'm sorry to be a weepy diva."

"Hey, you're beautiful and pregnant, we'll forgive you anything." Brock winked at Jesse.

She smiled and buried her face in Allie's neck. Emotion swelled up in her so big it overflowed her heart to fill every part of her.

She loved Brock. Head-over-heels, gaga-eyed, deep-end-of-the-pool, out-of-her-depth in love.

"Are you all right?" Brock said in her ear.

His heat surrounded her, and his hand settled in the familiar spot on her waist. His concern, as much as his closeness, warmed her. He touched her on so many levels. She was so lucky to have him in her life.

And so screwed.

His misguided view of his culpability in his fiancée's death made him afraid to commit. If she couldn't convince him that he wasn't to blame for the accident, there'd be no future for them.

But she wouldn't think of that tonight. He'd gone to a lot of trouble to make tonight special.

For her.

How he found out about her birthday she didn't know. But he was the first person to ever go out of his way to make her feel special.

"I'm wonderful. Thanks to you." She turned into the circle of his arms, Allie cradled between them. She stood on tiptoe and kissed him softly on the mouth. "Whatever else you have planned, tonight has already been exceptional."

He grinned. "You haven't seen anything yet, sweetheart." He pulled her to him for a harder, deeper kiss. "Go get fancied up. We leave in half an hour."

The rest of the night provided further proof of Brock's mastery of logistics and his attention to detail. From the champagne limo ride, to the window table at the Ocean View restaurant, and the moonlit ride in the horse-drawn carriage, everything was perfect.

And best of all, everything was about her.

"This has been the best day ever," she said to Brock in the limo on the way home. She rested her head on his shoulder and snuggled close. "It's odd how you never seem to get around to exploring the city you live in."

"Yeah, I've seen you glancing at the carriages when we've passed them, and I guess it struck me that I've traveled the world, been to a lot of exotic ports, but never really explored my own hometown. It's been fun."

"Yeah." She giggled, "I'm sure you've always wanted to ride around downtown San Diego in a tassel-draped carriage."

He laughed and tipped up her head to kiss her. "The company made it worth it."

"I loved it." Grinning, she kissed him back. Then pulling back, she cupped his cheek in her hand. She wanted him to know how much tonight meant to her. "Thank you. Nobody has ever done anything this wonderful for me. You made me feel special and important and cared for."

"You are special," he assured her, his gaze holding hers, reflecting his sincerity. "And important and I do care about you."

Jesse bit her lip, her newly acknowledged feelings for him overflowing her heart. She wanted to tell him, but emotion swelled up to block her throat. Plus, he wasn't ready. But caring was a start, caring could lead to bigger and better feelings.

"And—" Brock reached up to press the button closing the partition between them and the driver "—the night is not over. It's about to get a whole lot more special."

He buried his mouth in the curve of her neck, sending a thrill skidding down her spine. She moaned and tilted her head to the side, offering him better access to the skin he sought.

"Hmm. You're not suggesting anything naughty, are you?"

"Of course not." He nibbled his way to the black spaghetti strap of her dress and pushed it off her shoulder with his mouth. "Just another ride."

* * *

Jesse pushed open the door of Sullivans' Jewels La Jolla store and stepped into an upscale yet welcoming storefront. Dark woods and gleaming glass with antique lines gave the impression of Old-World comfort. Crystal lighting and plush carpeting added the final touch of elegance.

Brock had an appointment with his commanding office this morning so Jesse finally had a chance to get his watch fixed.

A young blonde woman in a sharp red suit stepped forward with a genuine smile. "Welcome to Sullivans'. I'm Gabrielle. How can I help you."

"I was told Sullivans' specializes in the sale and repair of antique pocket watches." Jesse reached in her purse for Brock's watch. "My husband cherishes this piece, but it got broken in a recent accident. I'd like to see if it can be fixed."

"Certainly. Step this way."

Gabrielle led the way to a glass counter. Three rows of new and antique watches were on display. Many, she noticed, were quite distinctive.

"I'll see if Martin is in." Gabrielle picked up a phone and dialed an extension. "He does watch repairs for all our stores."

A few minutes later Martin, a man of indeterminate age, with thinning brown hair and sharp gray eyes, joined them at the counter and picked up Brock's watch.

He studied the watch intently, including the back where no damage was evident. Not looking up he said,

"The crystal will be easy to replace. I'll have to open the watch up to assess the internal damage. It's probably the main spring or balance staff. We handle repairs right on-site and have most of the parts on hand. It's a fine piece. Where did you get this watch?"

"My husband got it from his grandfather." Knowing from her mother's interest in antiques that the origin could add to the value of an object, Jesse had no problem answering the question.

"And the *S* stands for the family name?"

"I think so. His name is Sullivan, like the store here." She smiled to show she appreciated the connection but knew it had no real meaning. "But I'm afraid I don't know the full history. I do know it means a lot to him."

Martin nodded. "It's a fine piece," he repeated. "I'm going to take it into the back, open it up, then I'll be able to give you an estimate."

"Okay." Jesse watched him disappear through a door. Gabrielle asked if she could show Jesse anything else. Jesse shook her head. "I'll just browse while I wait."

The store held some stunning pieces, but she'd only roamed for a few minutes when a tall, dark-haired man in a black suit walked up to her.

"Mrs. Sullivan? I'm Rick Sullivan, president of Sullivans' Jewels."

"Hello." Jesse shook his hand, struck by his vivid blue eyes. He reminded her a lot of Brock; maybe there was a connection between the families somewhere in the past.

"Martin showed me the watch you brought in. I

collect antique railroad watches so he knew I'd be interested. He said your husband's name is Sullivan."

"Yes. Brock Sullivan. He's in the Navy. He broke the watch in an accident onboard ship."

"So he's out to sea, then?" Rick Sullivan relaxed against the counter and crossed his arms over his chest. "That must be hard for you."

"It is hard when he's away, but actually he's home now."

"Good. That's good." He seemed genuinely pleased to hear the news. "Do you think he'd be interested in selling the watch?"

"Oh, no." She shook her head, understanding now what his interest was. "It's a family piece. He was very upset when it was damaged in the accident. I'm actually surprising him by getting it fixed."

"So he doesn't know you've brought it here?" Sullivan asked, his casual tone at odds with his intent gaze.

"No. A friend recommended your store. And it was easy to remember with the name connection and all." Jesse began to wonder about the questions, but Gabrielle arrived with an estimate and a receipt and Sullivan straightened from his relaxed pose.

"You won't be disappointed," he assured her. "Martin is the best in the city. Gabrielle, make sure the Sullivans get the family discount."

"Oh, no," Jesse protested. "I didn't mean to imply any relationship."

"It's the least we can do for one of our country's servicemen." With a nod the man turned and walked away.

"Hey, man, thanks for today." Jake shook Brock's hand as they stood on the step outside the front door. "I hate this baby shower business, but Jesse's idea of a barbecue combined with the shower worked out fine. Emily is ecstatic with all the stuff she got."

"Yeah." Brock grinned at his friend. "I can see you're excited, too."

"Hey." Jake held up both hands in surrender. "She's eight months pregnant. Anything that makes her happy right now excites me twice as much." He slapped Brock on the back. "We're lucky men, we've got a couple of great ladies."

"Yeah." Thinking of the uninhibited loving of the night before, of Jesse's unstinting effort for their friends today, Brock agreed. "We sure do."

"I've got to tell you I was worried when you married so soon before our deployment sixteen months ago. I thought you were pulling one of your Galahad moves, but when I see the two of you together, you fit."

"We fit?" Brock liked the sound of that, more than he had any right to, considering his anticommitment philosophy.

"Yeah, it's obvious she makes you happy, man."

"And what about Jesse?" he wondered aloud. "Does she seem happy?"

"You'd know better than me, but I can tell you, she

glows when she looks at you. She either loves you a whole bunch or she's pregnant again."

Another comment which should have put the fear of God in him. Instead he felt an undeniable thrill. Which scared him to death.

"You're just saying that because you want someone to share the misery," he told Jake.

"Some, yeah." Jake laughed as he shook his head. "Except, it's not all misery, and she does love you. One thing's for sure, life should be a lot better now you've got the cast off. You must be loving that."

"Lord, yes. Physical therapy is torture, but the therapist is optimistic. He says the leg is strong and with hard work and patience I'll get full mobility back."

"Sweet, man. I never doubted."

"Daddy." Troy ran up to tug on Jake's arm. "Mom says to come on. She's gotta pee."

"Well, those are my marching orders." Jake headed down the walkway. "Give Jesse a kiss for me."

"Not on your life. I'm keeping all her kisses for myself."

Incredible. He had it bad. And he couldn't even bring himself to worry about it.

Brock stood on the step after the Reeds pulled away and contemplated what Jake said. Jesse did make Brock feel lucky. She'd given him something he hadn't had in eighteen years—a home.

He'd been on so many deployments over the years he'd lost count. This was the first time he'd felt he'd left someone important behind. Yet her daily e-mails, cards, letters and care packages kept him connected, so he felt involved in her life.

Going through Allie's development, birth and growth with Jesse had been an amazing experience. She'd been so free with her feelings, her fears, her excitement; she just drew him in. He learned to love Allie before she was ever born.

And that same generosity of spirit, Jesse's openness and humor, made every day onboard ship a little less lonely. She had good instincts where people were concerned. More than once he appreciated advice she gave him in dealing with problems.

More than a year ago Brock left behind a broken flower, but he'd returned to a blooming rose. Being a mother agreed with Jesse. No longer a girl, her intelligence and spirit made for a confident, self-assured woman. A very sexy woman.

He cared about Jesse. Lusted after her. She deserved everything good and wonderful in life, as did her daughter. But was he what was best for them?

History said no, but he wasn't ready to walk away just yet.

Jake said it; they fit. For now that was enough for Brock.

He turned to step inside, to go claim his kiss when a new voice hailed him, a voice he recognized all too well.

"Brock Sullivan, I want to talk to you."

CHAPTER TWELVE

BROCK turned to find his brother Rick walking up his drive. And across the street his twin, Rett, parked his Jaguar at the çurb, then he, too, headed for Brock.

Damn, they looked good. Identical except for style and personality, they had the Sullivan coloring of dark hair and blue eyes.

They were a sight for sore eyes and a complication he didn't need right now. He hadn't told Jesse about his family yet. And he really needed to do so before introductions became necessary.

Unfortunately, time had just run out.

"Rick, Rett," Brock greeted them. "What are you doing here?"

"We heard that you were in town, that you were hurt. Of course we came." Rick hauled Brock into his arms for a solid hug. "At least you're all in one piece."

"Ford squealed didn't he?" Brock figured his youngest brother must have imparted the news of his accident. "He should have told you I'm fine. No need to worry."

"Ford knew you were injured?" Rett demanded as he traded places with Rick, also giving Brock a hug before stepping back and surveying him from head to foot. "I'll have to beat him up later. You going to keep us on the doorstep here, or are you going fo invite us in to meet your bride?"

"I can't believe you got married without telling us." Rick shook his head in mock disappointment. "Gram is going to have some words for you."

Okay, no lie there.

"Gram," Brock muttered, love and shame battling for his emotions. He loved her so much, owed her so much, had disappointed her, oh, so much.

He realized with both anticipation and dread he'd have to go see her, now his brothers knew he was in town.

"Listen, guys, I'm going to need a few minutes before you come inside. But first, if Ford didn't tell you, how'd you know where to find me? How do you know about Jesse?"

Rick pulled a gold pocket watch from his pocket. "Your wife brought this into Sullivans' to be fixed."

"My watch." Brock reached for the timepiece. "I wondered where it went. Hey, it's working."

Behind him the door opened and Jesse stuck her head out. "What's going on out here?"

Busted. Damn. He'd really hoped for a few minutes to talk to her before having to make introductions.

"Mr. Sullivan." Jesse looked at Rick, then stepped

outside to join Brock on the doorstep. "What are you doing here?" She saw the watch in Brock's hand, and confusion and a touch of annoyance clouded her gaze. "I didn't expect you to deliver the watch. In fact, it was supposed to be a surprise."

Rick smiled and shrugged. "Believe me, it was a surprise."

"I don't understand." But she caught on fast. She shifted to get a better look at Rett. Brock saw her gaze move back and forth assessing the two men. "You're twins." Then her glance turned and nailed him. "Your brothers?"

"Yeah." Before he had a chance to explain further, more family arrived.

Ford and Cole appeared at the bottom of the walkway, and across the street Brock saw Alex pull to the curb in a black Escalade. Gram, Brock's cousin Mattie and Alex's wife, Samantha, all climbed from the vehicle.

What was going on here? The whole family minus kids had arrived on his doorstep. Emotion choked him. For so long he'd forced himself to stay away. He'd destroyed the safe world they all lived in, brought death and loss to the family. By staying away, he'd saved them the constant reminder of how he'd failed and disappointed them.

Why would they all seek him out?

"Brock?" Jesse stepped closer to her husband and wrapped her fingers around his arm. Who were all these people?

Family, obviously, the resemblance between them all confirmed that. But where had they all come from? Why had Brock not told her of them?

He removed her fingers from his arm and, holding her hand in his, raised their clasped hands to his heart. He looked down at her and she saw he shared some of her confusion, but so many more emotions clouded his blue eyes she couldn't begin to know what he felt.

"Come with me," he said, "there's someone I want you to meet." Hand in hand, he led her past his brothers to meet a petite, gray-haired woman with alert blue eyes.

"Gram." He let go of Jesse to give the older woman a hug, then stepped back and drew Jesse forward. "Gram, this is my wife, Jesse." When he went on, he didn't quite meet Jesse's gaze. "This is my grandmother."

"My dear." Gram reached for Jesse's hand, squeezed and held on. "I'm so glad to meet you." Gram sent Brock a chiding glance. "I'm quite upset with Brock for keeping you a secret."

Grandmother. Jesse swallowed hard. Further introductions followed. More brothers, a cousin, sister-in-law. So many people, so much family.

What a fool she felt. She'd thought Brock alone in the world. Thought she'd given him something all these months that he'd lacked in his life.

Numb with shock, she pasted a smile on her face. "Everyone, please come inside. I'm sure you all have a lot of catching up to do."

She began to back away, almost bumped into a towering brother. Cole or was it Ford? "Excuse me. I have to check on Allie. Please come inside."

Desperately needing a moment to compose herself, she turned and fled. She didn't stop until she reached Allie's room. The baby slept soundly, exhausted after all the activity at the barbecue earlier.

Jesse wished for the sweet release of oblivion. Perhaps then she could deny the pain of betrayal, could pretend the past few minutes were nothing more than a nightmare.

The opposite of the last month or so, which had been a dream come true.

For six weeks Brock had been attentive and affectionate. Ever since her birthday, she'd really felt they'd become a family. She'd known better than to allow herself to believe in a future with Brock, but he'd been so loving that her heart won the argument over her head.

But loving and love were not the same.

He wouldn't have hidden his family from her if he loved her.

Not once had he mentioned his brothers or cousin to her. And when he'd spoken of his past, of Gram and of Sherry, Jesse got the impression both were just that, a part of his past.

What was it about her that was so unlovable? Why didn't she deserve to be part of a family?

Tears welled up, filling her eyes, but she refused to blink, refused to let them fall. She snagged a tissue from the changing table and dried her eyes.

She looked down at Allie and realized she was her family, the only person in the world who loved her.

Jesse wasn't the one losing anything here. From the beginning she'd known Brock wasn't hers to keep. Because of him she had a healthy, beautiful baby girl. And if he didn't want the two of them in his life, the loss was his.

One tear escaped to land on Allie's arm. The baby's eyes opened and she rolled over to look up at Jesse. She didn't cry, but neither did she go back to sleep. As if sensing Jesse's sadness, she sat up and lifted her arms to her mother to be picked up. "Mama."

"Baby." Jesse held the tiny body to her, absorbing all the love and acceptance communicated by the grip of small arms and the laying of Allie's head on Jesse's shoulder. "I love you."

"Jesse." Brock stood in the doorway.

"We're coming." Ashamed of the husky sound of her voice, she kept her head averted, unwilling to let him see her tears.

"I want to talk to you first. To explain." He stepped closer.

"That can wait." She moved away, still not looking at him, reaching instead for Allie's toy elephant. "You have company."

"That's what I want to talk to you about. I know you're upset because I didn't tell you about my family. But that's because of me. It has nothing to do with you."

"We need to rejoin your guests." She walked around him to the hall doorway. "Your family is waiting."

He caught her arm, stopping her. "You and Allie are my family."

"Please don't say that." She didn't fight him, didn't pull away. She bowed her head and said, "Don't say something you don't mean just to make me feel better. That's not fair to either of us."

Cradling Allie close, Jesse joined the horde of Sullivans in the living room. She sat down next to Gram on the sofa. As she expected, the attention shifted from her to Allie. The women gathered around to coo over her.

Jesse let Brock answer their questions. He'd always given the impression Allie was his, but she'd understand if he chose not to continue that facade with his family. The choice was his.

She wouldn't lie to his family.

Proud as a true papa, he provided Allie's vital statistics, followed by her every accomplishment.

"She's starting to pull herself up on the furniture and shimmy along. It won't be long before she's walking."

"Brock, she's wonderful." When she went on, Gram's tone held a note of sadness. "Why have you held yourself apart from us so long?"

He remained expressionless. "The Navy tends to require long absences."

Gram shook her head but allowed the evasion.

Jesse felt the obvious love in the room, and it distressed her to see the family torn apart by Brock's detachment.

The conversation continued as the family caught up on news of each other. Of course they were curious about the details of Jesse and Brock's marriage. With sixteen months of experience, Jesse easily fielded the questions.

"We're glad to have him home," she said after providing a few details, deliberately focusing on the present to distract them from the past. "We've been celebrating the removal of his cast the past couple of days."

This comment moved the discussion to Brock's accident and the status of his injury. His brothers showed concern in the way of all men, joking with him about his limitations.

"This may end up being the best thing to happen to me," Brock spoke up. He looked directly at Jesse. "I find I love spending time at home with my wife and daughter."

Later that night Jesse lay on her side in bed facing away from Brock. Confused by the events of the evening and wanting time to think, she'd evaded him after his family left by busying herself putting Allie to sleep. And then Jesse hopped into bed while he showered and pretended to be asleep when he joined her.

Why hadn't he told her about his family?

Her mind worried at the question like her tongue played with a sore tooth, she couldn't leave it alone no matter how much it hurt to touch.

The Sullivans had finally departed, en masse just as

they had arrived. They were good people, obviously concerned about their missing link.

Jesse particularly noticed the tension and hurt in Gram and Alex, Brock's older brother, as if they took the estrangement more personally than the others.

No matter how she reasoned, Jesse couldn't understand why Brock distanced himself from such a large, caring family. She knew it must have something to do with the accident that resulted in Sherry's death, but none of the Sullivans appeared to harbor resentment against Brock.

Had he ostracized himself in self-punishment?

Sherry lost her life so he must also lose something of great value?

So where did that leave Jesse? Was she merely a good deed his sense of honor demanded in exchange for the disasters of his youth?

The very thought of being reduced to a duty in Brock's eyes devastated Jesse. She'd lived through that demeaning existence once and had vowed never to put herself in such a position again.

In the midst of the Sullivans today, she'd felt like an outsider looking in, but she'd still found more warmth and welcome from Brock's family than she did from her own. Their kindness and genuine interest in getting to know her touched her deeply.

And they all lived within forty miles of here. So close, and yet so far out of reach.

Why hadn't Brock told her about them?

Or maybe the question should be why did she expect that he would? After all, she'd been nothing to him when he took her in. And they'd made their arrangement with no expectation that she'd ever be anything to him except an ex-wife who lived in his condo while he was away.

But for all that that was true, he'd rarely been distant or alienating in his behavior. Instead he treated her with respect and concern; more, he acted as if he cared, introducing her to his friends, sending SEALs out to make sure she was safe, traveling halfway around the world for Allie's birth.

Oh, Lord. Had her childhood screwed her up more than she knew? Had she mistaken simple courtesy and an amazing generosity of spirit for affection and an emotional connection?

In her mind she'd been building a future together for them. A home, children, becoming a family.

While in his mind she didn't even rate an introduction to his family.

She loved him yet suddenly she didn't know if the chemistry between them was anything more than lust on his side. The uncertainty scared her to death.

Behind her Brock rolled to his side and the heat of his hand settled on her hip.

She flinched, afraid to believe in the sincerity of his touch.

"I know you're awake," he said softly. "And I know you're upset, but you have to believe me, the reason I didn't tell you about my family has everything to do with me and nothing to do with you."

"How does that make it better?" she whispered in the dark. "You've shut me out of a huge part of your life. Either I'm not important enough to you to warrant an introduction, or you don't trust me. I'm not sure which is worse."

"Neither is true. I'm at fault. I warned you I'd disappoint you."

Now, that fired her blood. She rolled from the bed and turned to confront him.

"That is such a crock. Do you think I can't see you're hurting? Do you think it doesn't matter to me? If you're so afraid of disappointing me, talk to me. Explain to me why it's necessary to distance yourself from your family. It's obvious you love each other."

"And pain cuts sharpest the ones we love." He rolled to his back, stared up at the ceiling. "But I'm not noble enough to leave for their sakes. I'm not that strong. I left because I couldn't stand to see the contempt in their eyes."

"I saw the way they look at you, Brock. Whatever happened in the past, there was nothing but love in that room tonight."

"Right." He scooted up so he sat against the headboard. A scowl showed his rising temper. "But then you don't exactly have experience with loving families, do you?"

The impact of that statement had her stumbling back as if she'd taken a punch to the jaw.

Wow, she never saw the shot coming. Pain burned through her even as she recognized on another level how uncharacteristic the attack was. Too hurt to care, she refused to show him how the comment affected her.

She'd married a military man; she shouldn't be surprised when he came out fighting. Usually she dealt with the protective side of the warrior. Not this time. Like any cornered animal, he struck out when in pain.

Blinded by the past, wounded both in body and spirit, he'd had a lot to deal with lately. And having his family arrive on his doorstep obviously upset him.

She didn't know what to do, but she did know she was in the middle of a life-and-death battle.

The future of her marriage hinged on the outcome of this confrontation. Because if Brock couldn't put the past behind him, they had no future.

Chin up, she crossed her arms over her chest and reclaimed the ground she'd lost.

"You're right, I have no experience with loving families. Which is why I can recognize it when I see it. And let me tell you, there are worse things than contempt. Disinterest for one. Loneliness for another, so I have plenty of experience in that regard."

She swept a hand through her hair.

"Maybe I've got this wrong, maybe the problem isn't with you but with your family. They reached out to you today, but what happened in the past? Did they hurt you beyond forgiveness?"

"Now you're talking nonsense. I told you I killed the

woman I loved. Nobody could blame them for viewing me with contempt. Least of all me."

Frustrated, she continued to push. "Do you love your family?"

"Of course." The sharpness of his tone showed the edge of his temper.

"If it had been one of them driving Sherry, would you have turned on them?"

He frowned, obviously affronted by the question. "Of course not."

"Yet you think it was so easy for them to blame you."

"I know Alex did." The words burst out of him as if released under pressure. She wondered how long he'd held the resentment inside. "I heard him in the hospital after I was brought in. He ranted about my stupidity for driving in bad conditions, for allowing Sherry to influence my judgment."

"Brock, he was in shock." Jesse stopped, realized she needed to calm down, too, and drew in a deep breath. "You said you heard him. Did you ever talk to him about it?"

He sent her a sharp glance. "I didn't need to hear it again. Once was enough."

She sighed and sat on the edge of the bed, her leg half curled under her so she faced Brock. "You can't hold him accountable for what he said in the heat of the moment. He'd just lost a friend, and he almost lost you. All that emotion needed an outlet. He was probably railing more at the situation than at you."

She laid her hand on his sheet-covered knee. "He had

to be scared and relieved, angry, grieving, heck he probably blamed himself for the accident when he was no more responsible for the deer being in the middle of the road than you were."

"Would you just let the whole accident thing go?" He leaned his head back against the headboard, covered his eyes with his forearm. "It's ancient history. Not important."

"I can't let it go, because it is important and because you haven't let it go. It was horrible and it was tragic but it was an accident."

Distressed by his lack of response, by her inability to reach him, Jesse stood to pace.

"Do you still love her?" She forced the question out. "Is that why you can't let the past go?"

A harsh laugh escaped him. "God, you're relentless. You want the truth? It kills me, but I don't even remember what she looked like."

She heard the pain in his voice, the desperation. "It was eighteen years ago," she reminded him. "It's understandable for the memories to fade." A thought struck her. "Is that why you've focused your whole life on atonement for that one event? So you wouldn't forget?"

"I've spent the past eighteen years in the Navy. Believe me there was no time for atonement."

"But you were in college prior to the accident. You quit to join the Navy. You watch out for your crew as if they were family but shut yourself away from the family you love. That sounds like atonement to me."

"Well, you're wrong." The sharpness of his denial convinced her she'd hit the mark.

"Brock, you're the best man I know. And you may deny it, but you blame yourself for Sherry's death. Unconsciously you've been trying to make up for it ever since. Well, you can stop. If there is such a thing as a cosmic trade-off of a life for a life, you don't have to look any further than the nursery down the hall. Actually, you don't have to look any further than me.

"You saved me that night at the Green Garter. I was young, scared and stupid. And very much alone. When I think about how close I came to losing Allie, I die a little inside. You saved her life and you saved mine. I'm no longer that lonely, frightened girl. I have a job, friends, a beautiful baby and self-respect. You gave me all of that and I'll always be grateful."

She suddenly found herself looking into intense blue eyes. "I don't want your gratitude, Jesse."

"Too bad, because you'll always have it. You gave me my life back. You believed in me, so I was able to believe in myself, to regain my self-esteem. I've put the insecurities of my childhood behind me. So, yeah, I'm grateful, but that's only one emotion among many. I love you, Brock."

She didn't know what reaction she expected, but his expressionless silence unnerved her. Her heart beat wildly as she waited for a response. She swallowed hard; maybe she'd misread his level of emotional commitment these past few weeks.

"Say something." She prompted him, hating the shake in her voice. "Today you told your family you love spending time with your wife and daughter." From the way he'd looked at her at the time, she'd thought he'd been trying to tell her something. As the seconds ticked by and dread filled her chest, she experienced serious doubts.

Before her eyes his expression went from blank to dead cold.

"What was I supposed to tell them, that I've hooked up with a stranger who doesn't know when to leave?"

CHAPTER THIRTEEN

BROCK immediately wished the words back. He watched Jesse go white, watched her digest the rejection and felt her pain as his own.

He loved her. It hit him fast and hard. For all he'd tried to keep his distance—and failed—for all he'd told himself she deserved better, that he'd only hurt her, he'd had no real control of his fate.

He loved Jesse.

And he'd just told her she meant nothing to him.

Obviously stricken, she backed away from the bed.

"Jesse, I'm sorry." Brock swung his legs off the bed. His left foot hit the floor with a thud, and pain ricocheted through his mostly healed leg. He ignored it, punching to his feet. "I didn't mean that."

She just shook her head, steadily backing away. At the dresser she jerked jeans from a drawer, quickly yanking them on, then she grabbed a sweater and headed for the door.

Fear consumed him as he realized she was leaving. Not just the room, but the house. Him.

He moved fast, but she moved faster. Hampered by his weakened leg, by the time he reached the hall, she'd already swept up Allie and a diaper bag and headed for the front door.

"Jesse, please stop." He reached her, caged her body between him and the door, his front to her back, Allie secure in her arms. "Don't leave like this," he whispered against her ear. "You know I didn't mean it."

"You said it." She stood stiff and unyielding in the circle of his arms. "You must have meant it on some level."

"No, you and Allie are the best things that ever happened to me. That's the only thing I'm truly sure about right this minute. I just—"

He faltered, uncomfortable with admitting to a weakness. But either he opened up or he would lose any hope of a happy future. Resting his forehead on the soft warmth of her hair, he took strength from her closeness. Only complete honesty could save him now. "You kept poking at the past and it's like this huge open wound inside me. You got too close and I lashed out."

"I was trying to help."

"I know, and a lot of what you said made sense, but I wasn't ready to listen, to act. It's a lot to take in, to consider. You need to give me time. Please. Don't leave."

"I have to go. I've fought too hard to reach this point in my life." The words were a shaky whisper. "I won't give up my self-respect again. Not even for you."

"Jesse." It broke his heart to hear how low he'd brought her. "Please."

The tension went out of her, but she didn't turn.

"You do have a lot to think about. Your future with the Navy, the past, us. Take the time you need. And then we'll talk."

She opened the door and he had no choice but to let her go. The hardest thing he'd ever do was watch her walk over the threshold out of his life.

She paused briefly. "Think hard, Brock, because if you can't put the past away, Sherry's death wasn't just wrong and sad, the real tragedy will be that the accident stole not only her life but yours, as well."

Sunday dinner at Gram's. It was a tradition Brock remembered from before his parents died. He and Alex had supported Gram's insistence on continuing it after their parents' deaths as a way to keep the family unit strong.

Brock climbed the stairs to the porch of Gram's Victorian manor in Paradise Pines. It felt odd to knock, but odder still to just walk in, so he knocked.

After a moment Ford opened the door. His youngest brother took one look at Brock and broke into a grin.

"It's about time." Ford hauled Brock into a huge hug. "Come on in. We're all here just as you requested. Hey, I heard they transferred you to Coronado, home of the SEALs. Congratulations."

"Yeah." Brock sent his brother a rueful glance. "You wouldn't have anything to do with that would you?"

"I knew the master chief was planning to retire at the end of this year. I just mentioned you might be interested in shore duty now you've started a family."

"It's a prestigious position." This part, at least, was easier than Brock anticipated. The clear bill of health along with the new assignment resolved all his anxiety for his future with the Navy. Not only did his superiors consider him fit, they wanted him to go for master chief the next go around. "Thanks, man."

"Hey, you earned it." Ford ushered Brock inside the foyer. "I just let them know you were available. We're back in the kitchen just like always. I'm anxious for you to meet my wife, Rachel, and the twins."

Brock had never seen the kitchen so packed with people. Introductions were a jumble of names and faces. He met Rachel and was reintroduced to Samantha, his sisters-in-law and a number of nieces and nephews. Gram held center stage at the big butcher-block table.

His last visit had been to Alex's wedding the month before Brock met Jesse. And that had been in Las Vegas.

Home. It was all so different, yet so much the same. Warm and welcoming. Except for the new faces, it felt like he'd never left.

A hand landed on his shoulder. He turned to come face-to-face with Alex. His older brother cocked his head toward the back porch. "Let's talk."

"Yeah, let's." Brock led the way. He wanted his

family back, and so far they were making it easy, but to make it last he needed to have the talk with Alex he'd walked away from eighteen years ago.

On the porch they both leaned against the white railing that overlooked Gram's rose garden.

"I hope this visit means we'll now be seeing you for Sunday dinners," Alex said.

"Maybe," Brock answered. "That depends on you."

"Me?" Alex turned to face Brock. "Why on me?"

Brock told Alex what he heard that night in the hospital eighteen years ago. "All these years I've thought you blamed me for the accident. You said so that night, that I disappointed you by not acting responsibly."

"Brock." Alex shook his head. "I don't remember much about that night except losing Sherry and almost losing you. I was so scared yet still trying to keep it together for Gram and the boys."

He swept a hand through his hair. "Yeah, I remember now, you hadn't woken up yet, but the room had cleared out. Cole was keeping Sherry's parents advised of your status and Gram took the younger boys to the cafeteria. I looked at you in that bed—broken and bruised with tubes and machines hooked up to you—and I lost it.

"You were my best friend, always there when I needed you. And when you needed me most, there was nothing I could do. I wasn't talking to you at all but to myself." Alex wrapped an arm around Brock, dragging him close until their heads butted. "Damn, I'm sorry. I never knew you heard me, never realized you took it all to heart."

"I'll be damned." Brock pressed his head against Alex's, holding him close. Love overwhelmed him and he felt a nine-ton weight lift off his shoulders. "Jesse was right."

"Why didn't you talk to me?" Alex demanded as he stepped back. "I knew you blamed yourself for the accident. It didn't occur to me you thought I blamed you, too. Is that why you joined the Navy right after you got out of the hospital?"

Brock nodded. "I couldn't handle losing Sherry and your respect, too. And I couldn't just go back to school and pretend nothing had changed."

"It's been eighteen years. Brock, you ass, why didn't you talk to me?"

Brock lifted and dropped one shoulder. "At first I had to bury it to cope. It hurt too much to think about home without remembering Sherry and how I disappointed you. It was all connected in my mind. Jesse says I've spent all these years atoning for my sins."

"Those sound like fighting words. Does this have anything to do with your call asking the family to meet you here today?"

Brock cleared his throat, feeling sheepish. "Well, about that…I need the family to do me a favor."

Jesse paced Emily's small guest room. Allie slept peacefully in a day crib set up in the corner, happy as long as Jesse was near.

She knew just how Allie felt, because she was completely unhappy without Brock.

Which hardly made sense as they'd spent more time apart than together for the length of their relationship. She had, however, kept her promise to him to write every day. He'd been slow to respond at first but once he did he'd opened up and they'd really gotten to know each other.

Perhaps that's what made the difference. They'd become friends before they became lovers. Which made her doubly miserable.

She missed her friend, longed for her lover.

Yet she still heard the echo of him calling her a stranger. How that hurt.

He said he'd lashed out in pain and anger. Well, her warrior knew how to hit his target.

It didn't matter that he immediately regretted saying it. Didn't matter that she knew, truly knew, he didn't mean the upsetting comment. After all, actions—sixteen months' worth—did speak louder than words.

What mattered was she'd spent too many years as a stranger in her own home to pretend the hurtful words were never said.

She'd barely slept the night before, and her mind reeled from the same thoughts playing again and again. She'd hoped, irrationally, that Brock would be on Emily's doorstep first thing this morning to tell her he loved her and couldn't live without her and Allie. Demanding she come home.

But that had been her ego at work.

Since then she'd had time to think, and she didn't want a quick visceral reaction from him about getting back what was lost. She wanted a thoughtful response that meant his mind and heart were ready to commit to a future together.

Did she want Brock in her life? Yes, but only if it was what he truly wanted, not just his standard take-the-world-on-his-shoulders mind-set.

A knock sounded at the bedroom door. Emily. Her friend had been a rock, opening her home to Jesse in the middle of the night without question or hesitation. Emily hadn't even pushed Jesse for answers today, allowing her privacy to think and to cry. Now she thought of it, that was pretty unusual for Emily.

Jesse forced a smile for her understanding friend and opened the door. "Hey, did you get tired of my moping— Brock."

Her husband stood in the upstairs hall dressed in a white long-sleeved shirt rolled up to the elbows and straight-legged blue jeans. He looked casually masculine and powerfully male. Her heart smiled just seeing him. Her head warned her not to get ahead of herself.

"Jesse, can I come in?"

"Oh, my gosh, Brock. How did you make it up the stairs with your leg?"

His grin held an edge of determination. "Where there's a will there's a way."

"I could have come down."

"No." He shook his head and stepped forward, gently guiding her back into the room with a hand on her elbow. "It was important I come to you." He curved a hand around her neck and pulled her into his arms. "I missed you last night."

"I—" She swallowed a lump the size of a house, blinking to keep the tears at bay. How she longed to lay her head on his shoulder and pretend everything was all right. "I missed you, too."

He released her to limp over to the crib, softly stroking a thumb over Allie's cheek. "I missed you both." He looked up at Jesse. "I love her, Jesse. She's sweet and smart and funny. And so innocent. She reminds me why I go to work every day. She is my daughter, in my heart and in the eyes of the law, and I wouldn't have it any other way."

Jesse nodded; she had no doubts in that regard. It had been a love affair between the two of them from the very beginning. And for Brock it started before Allie was born.

"Before I say anything else I need to apologize. I know I hurt you with that crack about strangers last night."

She crossed her arms over her chest. "We went over that last night. You already apologized."

"I know. Jesse, I don't want you to believe there was any truth in it. Not a shred. I was hurting and angry and I knew it would hurt you. Not one of my finer moments, but I promise you I will never use your past as a weapon against you ever again."

His image swam before her eyes. A promise from Brock banked better than gold. Still she needed to make it clear.

"I can't be in another relationship where I'm an outsider."

He came to her again, cradled her face in his hands and spoke directly into her eyes.

"I joined the Navy because I needed to save someone, if in the most peripheral way. In the end the Navy saved me, first by giving me a purpose for living, then by giving me a haven, a home when I didn't feel I could face my family. And finally it gave me you, the mate of my soul."

"Oh, Brock."

"When I met you, work had taken over my life. I had forgotten what it meant to have a home, to have someone share their day and be able to tell them about mine. I let you live in my house, but you gave me a home and more. I hadn't realized how disconnected I'd become. There were days on ship when I felt I'd lose my mind except for the e-mail coming in from you.

"I love you, Jesse. You stopped me from saying it last night, and I'm glad because the timing was wrong, the moment ugly. Today is beautiful. Today is the first day of our future together. If you'll have me."

"Oh, Brock."

"You keep saying my name. Does that mean yes?"

She drew in a shaky breath, love and hope ready to break free inside her. "Are you sure?"

"Oh, yeah. My heart recognized you long ago. It just took my slow-witted mind and stubborn pride a while to catch up. Your youth and honesty, your sheer goodness meant you deserved better than this beat-up old sailor."

"Don't say that. You're the most vital, alive man I know."

"Well, it seems the Navy agrees with you to some extent. I got reassigned to Coronado. So I'll be here for both you and Allie."

Everything was falling into place. Almost too good to be true. But Brock didn't lie, and in his eyes she clearly saw love and sincerity.

She threw her arms around his neck and hugged him hard. "That's wonderful. When did this happen? It's Sunday."

"My commanding officer knew I was anxious for news, so he called me."

"No more deployments?"

"No more deployments. And I made up with Alex today. My day will be perfect if you'll agree to marry me for real."

"Oh, Brock."

"There's my name again." He kissed her, claiming her mouth with gentle persuasion. "I have a surprise that may help you make up your mind." Placing a warm hand in the small of her back he led her toward the window.

She stopped him, turned into his arms and pulled his

head down for another heated exchange. "I don't need any inducements. I love you, Brock. Nothing would make me happier than spending the rest of my life with you."

"It's about time." He grinned against her mouth then turned the caress into a tender celebration of love.

She leaned into him, happy to be home again. Because the one thing their separation taught her was home wasn't where she lived but within the circle of his arms.

"What's my surprise?"

He gestured out the window and she moved closer to look out over the backyard. Emily's small yard overflowed with men, women and children. Jesse saw Emily and Jake, Gram and Alex, Rick and his twin. Sullivans everywhere, big and little, young and old laughing and eating ice cream.

"Your family," she said in wonder. "They came with you."

"Our family," he corrected. "They came for you. You're one of us now."

"Oh, Brock."

Silhouette®

SPECIAL EDITION™

NEW YORK TIMES BESTSELLING AUTHOR

DIANA PALMER

A brand-new Long, Tall Texans novel

HEART OF STONE

Feeling unwanted and unloved, Keely returns to Jacobsville and to Boone Sinclair, a rancher troubled by his own past. Boone has always seemed reserved, but now Keely discovers a sensuality with him that quickly turns to love. Can they each see past their own scars to let love in?

Available September 2008
wherever you buy books.

SSE24921

"The more I see, the more I feel the need."

—**Aviva Presser,** real-life heroine

*Aviva Presser is a Harlequin More Than Words
award winner and the founder of **Bears Without Borders**.*

Discover your inner heroine!

⚓ HARLEQUIN
WWW.HARLEQUINMORETHANWORDS.COM

MTW07API

REQUEST YOUR FREE BOOKS!
2 FREE NOVELS PLUS 2
FREE GIFTS!

HARLEQUIN ROMANCE®

From the Heart, For the Heart

YES! Please send me 2 FREE Harlequin Romance® novels and my 2 FREE gifts (gifts are worth about $10). After receiving them, if I don't wish to receive any more books, I can return the shipping statement marked "cancel". If I don't cancel, I will receive 4 brand-new novels every month and be billed just $3.32 per book in the U.S. or $3.80 per book in Canada, plus 25¢ shipping and handling per book and applicable taxes, if any*. That's a savings of over 15% off the cover price! I understand that accepting the 2 free books and gifts places me under no obligation to buy anything. I can always return a shipment and cancel at any time. Even if I never buy another book, the two free books and gifts are mine to keep forever.

114 HDN ERQW 314 HDN ERQ9

Name	(PLEASE PRINT)	
Address		Apt. #
City	State/Prov.	Zip/Postal Code

Signature (if under 18, a parent or guardian must sign)

Mail to the Harlequin Reader Service:
IN U.S.A.: P.O. Box 1867, Buffalo, NY 14240-1867
IN CANADA: P.O. Box 609, Fort Erie, Ontario L2A 5X3

Not valid to current subscribers of Harlequin Romance books.

Want to try two free books from another line?
Call 1-800-873-8635 or visit www.morefreebooks.com.

* Terms and prices subject to change without notice. N.Y. residents add applicable sales tax. Canadian residents will be charged applicable provincial taxes and GST. This offer is limited to one order per household. All orders subject to approval. Credit or debit balances in a customer's account(s) may be offset by any other outstanding balance owed by or to the customer. Please allow 4 to 6 weeks for delivery. Offer available while quantities last.

Your Privacy: Harlequin Books is committed to protecting your privacy. Our Privacy Policy is available online at www.eHarlequin.com or upon request from the Reader Service. From time to time we make our lists of customers available to reputable third parties who may have a product or service of interest to you. If you would prefer we not share your name and address, please check here. ☐

HR08

HARLEQUIN Romance

Coming Next Month

Explore the rugged scenery of the Scottish Highlands, share the joys of first pregnancies and escape to the scorching heat of the desert this July in Harlequin Romance®!

#4033 PARENTS IN TRAINING by Barbara McMahon
Unexpectedly Expecting!
How exciting to finally have that longed-for baby! Concluding the inspiring duet, pregnant Annalise can't wait for babies with her husband. But although Dominic adores his wife, he always thought theirs would be a perfect family of *two....*

#4034 NEWLYWEDS OF CONVENIENCE by Jessica Hart
Corporate wife Mallory promised her new husband a businesslike marriage—no messy emotions involved! But moving to the Scottish Highlands where she discovers he's rugged, capable and utterly gorgeous, Mallory thinks she might want to break the terms of their arrangement.

#4035 WINNING THE SINGLE MOM'S HEART by Linda Goodnight
The Wedding Planners
Single moms like Natalie need romance, too! In this captivating story, competitive Cooper Sullivan is at the top of his career—but seeing Natalie after so many years, he realizes the only thing he really wants to win is her heart!

#4036 ADOPTED: OUTBACK BABY by Barbara Hannay
Baby on Board
Nell thought she'd missed her chance to be a mom when she was forced to put her baby up for adoption as a teenager. Now, at age thirty-nine, she discovers she has a tiny grandson who needs her! And the baby's grandfather, Nell's former sweetheart Jacob, is back in town....

#4037 THE DESERT PRINCE'S PROPOSAL by Nicola Marsh
Desert Brides
Prince Samman *must* marry to be crowned King—but he rejects all his advisors' suggestions! He wants intelligent, independent Bria Green, who's determined the powerful prince won't get his way. But will the scorching heat of the desert change her mind?

#4038 BOARDROOM BRIDE AND GROOM by Shirley Jump
9 to 5
What's your idea of the perfect date? Gorgeous lawyer Nick certainly doesn't think a children's picnic with prim colleague Carolyn is his! Yet Carolyn intrigues him, and Nick starts to think he has never seen anyone more beautiful....

HRCNM0608